PERRIN IN PERIL

A Perrin Inherent YA Fantasy

C. S. Dexter

CSD Digital Enterprises, LLC

Three people each paid for a copy of this book before it was finished being written. I am sure they have lost patience with me eleven years ago. For that is how long I have been struggling to get this book in a form that is agreeable to almost everyone. Therefore I dedicate this book to the three who have paid for it years ago:

Suzanne Foster
Michelle Jackson-Britton
Cary Taylor

And I also dedicate it to my daughter who originally came up with the characters and wanted the book set in Japan. Which hasn't happened yet.

Elise K. Dexter

CHAPTER 1: I AM REALLY STUPID

Perrin Roberts thinks her mother is some kind of spy. She has a job that she cannot talk about—*ever.* She gets phone calls where she speaks in code and then has to rush out. Perrin's grandma Grace Roberts lives with them and watches Perrin when her mom is at work. Her mother's and grandmother's conversations seem to be in code as well. At least, that's what Perrin thought.

While trying to decide whether to put up her light-brown hair with a ribbon or keep it down, Perrin heard her mother and grandmother talking as they passed her room.

"Have you told her yet, Pandra?" Perrin heard her Grandmother ask.

"Grace, I'm not ready to tell her," Pandra answered.

"The enemy has known this for thousands of years, so don't you think they would be ready by now?" Grace asked.

"They don't know who or where she is, let's drop this before she hears us," Pandra said nervously.

"You also didn't think they knew who or where Bill was before he disappeared. Thinking like that is dangerous and—

"SOMAF has got this all covered, Grace!" Pandra said with a firm whisper. "They've even got someone in the school watching her."

"The enemy does too, I bet," Grandma replied. "But Perrin—

"*PERRIN*, if you don't leave now for school, you're going to be late!" Pandra shouted down the hall.

"I know Mom," Perrin shouted back. "Just fixing my hair." Perrin usually listen in on conversations. But when the conversations are about her, she can't help but listen.

"I wonder what mom isn't ready to tell me?" Perrin whispered to herself. She tossed the ribbon on her dresser and quickly tried to curl her hair with a lukewarm curling iron.

"And who is watching me at school? And who is this *enemy* grandma is talking about?" Perrin asked herself in the mirror.

Lately, Perrin wonders if Grandma Roberts has gotten dementia. "Grandma says the strangest things to Mom and poor Mom has to deal with her."

Yet, sometimes Perrin can't tell which discussions they have come from dementia and which are real. "I'm pretty sure the '...enemy...,' comments were dementia."

The funny thing is, when her Grandmother talks to Perrin, she never hears a dementia-like comment.

"I am really stupid. At least that's what most kids at school say," said Perrin pulling the plug on her curling iron because it clearly wasn't working properly. *"The stupidest things happen wherever I go. I just can't seem to avoid it!"*

"Perrin, why did you say that?" Pandra asked. Perrin froze just as she was starting to reach for the front door.

"Did my thoughts come out of my mouth again?" Perrin asked knowing that she had done yet another stupid thing.

Pandra unhooked Perrin's backpack from the coat hooks on the wall and held it out to her. "Yes, your thoughts did, why?"

Perrin spun to face her and calmly took her backpack from her mother. "Because I think and do the stupidest things sometimes. Look, I was about to forget my backpack, which is another stupid thing I would've done."

"Saying that you are stupid, Perrin, is not good for your self-esteem," said Pandra.

"Mom, I don't think I have any self-esteem. I hardly have any presence on any social media site, and no one finds me popular. How can I have self-esteem if I don't have a ton of friends and boys fawning over me wherever I go."

"Perrin, self-esteem does not require social media, boys, or having lots of friends to praise your popularity. That's why they call it *self*-**esteem**. You have to believe in yourself and understand how incredible you are."

"Mom, I think you've forgotten what it's like to be

fourteen," Perrin said as she put on her backpack and turned, opening the front door. She stopped there out of habit because on the wall beside the door was a framed photo of her parents taken months before her father vanished. Perrin blew him a kiss. "Bye, Dad. I miss you," Perrin said. Then she walked out, closing the door behind her.

CHAPTER 2: THE BOY ON THE STEPS

Perrin Roberts balanced her phone at arm's length, tongue poking out in concentration as she tried to frame the shot just right. The screen showed the high school's brick entrance with its chipped paint and the giant metal stairs that funneled hundreds of kids inside every morning. What the shot didn't show was how utterly average she felt standing there, backpack slipping off her shoulder, her hair refusing to hold the curls she'd ironed in fifteen minutes earlier.

"Okay, followers," she whispered dramatically, pushing the red record button. "Today is the day your girl Perrin finally makes social history."

Her voice was swallowed by the chatter of students and the steady squeak of sneakers on wet pavement from over-watering school sprinklers. Most of the students barely noticed her — except Keri, who stood a few steps away tapping furiously on her phone. Keri was tall, all sharp elbows and quick sarcasm. Taloni leaned against the stair rail, head bobbing to music only she could hear, her dyed purple bangs hiding her eyes. Rosha, a girl whose family moved here from India last summer, was the newest to their friend group. Rosha adjusted the strap on her bookbag and gave Perrin a patient, almost motherly smile.

"Perrin," Rosha said gently, "the bell is going to ring in, what, three minutes? Maybe do this later?"

"No, no, the timing is perfect. Watch."

Perrin flipped her hair with all the confidence she could summon and hit record again. She wanted this video to be different from her usual ones — the ones people at school already mocked her for. Videos of her tripping in the hallway or mixing up song lyrics had gone semi-viral locally, but for the wrong reasons. She was tired of being a walking punchline. A living joke.

Today would change everything.

Because today, she had spotted him.

He'd just come through the crowd: tall, lean, and too good-looking to belong to a soggy Tuesday morning in Arizona. His eyes were pale gray, almost silver, and his blond hair fell just enough across his forehead to make him look like he didn't care how perfect it was. He didn't carry a backpack. He didn't even look nervous, which was suspicious in itself — new kids always looked nervous.

Perrin's heart thudded. "That's him. That's the boy."

Keri raised an eyebrow. "Which boy? Please don't say— oh. You mean tall, mysterious, and definitely out of your league?"

Perrin shot her a glare. "Shut up. He's perfect."

Taloni smirked without looking up from her earbuds. "Perfect usually means trouble."

But Perrin wasn't listening anymore. She lifted her phone higher and started narrating like she was some celebrity vlogger with a million fans hanging on her every word.

"Okay, people, this is Eric—" She didn't actually know his name yet, but this name popped up in her head, so she said it anyway. It felt right. "—and he's clearly new. Watch as I, Perrin Roberts, bravely investigate the mysterious transfer student. This is going to blow up my channel, guaranteed."

Eric moved smoothly through the crowd, and Perrin trailed after him with her phone raised. She was too focused on the shot to notice that she'd stepped off the curb.

Horns blared.

"Perrin!" Rosha shrieked.

She snapped her head up just in time to see the blinding headlights of a pickup truck bearing down on her. Perrin gasped and leapt sideways, her shoes skidding on the wet asphalt. She dodged one car only to stumble into the path of another.

"Move!" someone shouted.

She scrambled, hopping onto the hood of a third car to avoid being crushed between bumpers. Her phone was still recording the entire thing, every honk and curse word from the drivers. Students on the steps broke into laughter, pointing and pulling out their own phones to capture her humiliation.

Perrin's cheeks burned. She slid off the car's hood, muttered an apology to the furious driver, and darted back across the street to the school. Her friends were half-panicked, half-dying of laughter.

"Girl," Keri wheezed, "you're gonna end up on FailTube by third period."

"Already are," Taloni added, showing Perrin a livestream replaying the incident from another angle.

Perrin groaned. She never checked her videos before uploading them, a fatal flaw she somehow never learned from. By the time she thought about deleting it, her mistake would already be cemented in every classmate's feed.

Still, her embarrassment fizzled the second she realized who was waiting for her.

Eric stood at the top of the stairs, looking down at her with an expression that was equal parts amused and... curious. He hadn't pulled out his phone like everyone else. He hadn't laughed. He just stood there, his pale eyes locked on hers.

Perrin froze. For a moment, it felt like the entire schoolyard had gone silent.

Then Eric smiled. It wasn't big, not even warm — more like a secret. He lifted a hand, palm out, and beckoned her closer.

Her breath caught in her throat. Was this it? Was this the moment her life actually changed?

She climbed the stairs, fumbling to start recording again. If she was going to walk into the arms of her mysterious dream boy, she needed proof. Maybe her followers would finally see her as more than a disaster.

Eric's voice was soft when she reached him. "Keep filming."

The words slid into her ears like velvet, and Perrin's whole body tingled. She obeyed without thinking, camera raised, staring at him like she couldn't look away. His eyes seemed to deepen, pulling her in.

"You're mine now," he whispered.

The phone captured everything: the way her pupils dilated, the way her posture slumped as though she'd just agreed to something important, the faint smile that crept over his lips as he turned and walked into the building.

"Wait—" she breathed, but the word came out sluggish, like she'd forgotten how to move her own tongue.

Her friends rushed up behind her.

"What was that?" Keri demanded.

"You looked like you were in a trance," Rosha said.

But Perrin barely heard them. She was already replaying the moment in her head, replaying the smile, the command, the strange sense that she would do anything to follow him.

Anything.

And her phone had caught it all.

Perrin drifted through first period like she was walking underwater.

She tried to take notes. Her pen hovered. Words on the whiteboard refused to be words. Every time she blinked she saw the curve of Eric's mouth, the tilt of his head, the way her own body had answered his voice like a switch had been flipped at the base of her skull.

Second period wasn't better. Someone showed her the traffic clip that was already looping with a laughing skull emoji stamped across her face. She smiled like it didn't matter. Inside, she shrank.

By third period, she'd stopped pretending. She set her phone face-down and stared at the clock until the minute hand looked like it was crawling backward.

At lunch, the sun bounced off the damp patches the

sprinklers had left on the field, and the tables steamed. Keri and Taloni snagged a spot under the ragged shade of a dying palo verde; Rosha arrived with a neatly packed metal lunch box called a tiffin and a worried look.

"Okay," Keri said, ripping open a bag of chips. "Explain why you looked like a duckling imprinting on a lumberjack this morning."

"Lumberjack?" Taloni snorted. "He's more like a vampire who moisturizes."

Rosha set down her metal lunchbox. "You were... not yourself."

Perrin wanted to brush it off with a joke. Instead she picked at the corner of her tray. "He just—talked. And I felt—" She couldn't finish the sentence.

Rosha angled her head. "May I see the video?"

Perrin hesitated, then pushed her phone across the table. The clip from the stairs played: Eric's profile, that little hand motion, Perrin's face slipping from excited to empty like someone had turned down the lights behind her eyes.

Keri stopped chewing. "That's creepy."

"Not normal creepy," Taloni said. "Capital-C Creepy."

Rosha replayed the moment twice, then a third time, leaning so close the screen reflected in her irises. "He speaks a phrase," she murmured. "Not English. Not Spanish. The rhythm is old." She glanced up at Perrin. "My grandfather used to chant before ceremonies—different words, same cadence."

"So... what?" Keri said. "Maybe he's the son of a language teacher?"

Rosha ignored her. "There is a story from where I'm from—about a teacher of teachers. A name like shadow and moon." She fumbled for it, shook her head. "Never mind. Just—be careful."

"I am careful," Perrin said, even though the evidence—traffic clip, stair clip, her entire history—said otherwise.

Keri slid the phone back. "If you're going to keep filming, at least don't post without watching first. You're feeding the wolves."

Perrin nodded. She would absolutely not learn that lesson.

Math after lunch should have grounded her. Numbers didn't care if you were humiliated. Numbers were clean. But Mr. Gasker wasn't doing numbers today. He was doing show-and-tell.

"Goooood afternoon, statistical soldiers," he sang, slapping a dangling key fob against his palm. He was the kind of teacher who wore retro band tees with blazers and had posters of Mars landers and prewar race cars sharing the same bulletin board. "Anyone want to guess who had a very special morning?"

"Your therapist?" someone muttered.

"Close," he said cheerfully, then spun the fob on his

finger. "I had a meeting with a very important client from Space Tech Corporation." He let the name hang like he expected applause. A couple of kids did clap. "And because I am a paragon of responsibility—and because this campus is safer than my garage—I drove a little something to school."

He clicked his remote. The projector flashed an image of a low, predatory car shimmering in iridescent paint that shifted from iron blue to oil-slick green depending on the angle. The body looked like someone had carved it from a meteor. The rims were skeletal, the tires fat enough to eat speed bumps for breakfast.

Gasps. Actual gasps.

"It's in the lot," Gasker said, basking. "Prototype. Pre-pre-production. Custom powertrain. Experimental telemetry. And stuff so top secret, even aliens would be jealous. Don't touch it. Don't breathe on it. Don't think about it unless you've sanitized your brain."

"Is it street legal?" a boy in the back asked.

"For the next twenty-four hours only, because I signed ten forms," Gasker said. "But hear me, my children: if I come out and find so much as a fingerprint on that paint, I will personally weep on your transcripts."

Laughter. Phones came out. People whispered. Even the kids who hated cars craned to look at the projected beast.

Perrin didn't care—until the hairs along her arm lifted, and a cold thread tugged behind her sternum.

She didn't have to look to know he was there. He brushed past the open classroom door without slowing, just a shadow and a scent like metal and forest after rain —except there had been no rain, unless you counted the school sprinklers. The moment stretched. Mr. Gasker's voice receded to a muffled echo. The keys in his hand flashed like a signal.

You'll get Mr. Gasker's keys. Bring them to me.

Perrin's chest filled with helium. She sat up straighter, smiling without intending to. She raised her hand.

"Yes, Miss Roberts, a question?" Gasker said.

"Bathroom," she lied, and he waved her out, still talking about torque curves and nondisclosure agreements like the world hadn't just tilted on its axis.

In the hall, the air felt cooler. Eric leaned against the lockers opposite the math room, angled so anyone walking by would think he was waiting for a friend.

"You remember," he said softly.

She nodded. She couldn't not nod.

"Last bell," he murmured. "Bring me the keys."

He didn't touch her. He didn't need to. He winked —playful, almost kind—and strolled away, a ripple in the crowded hallway that people unconsciously moved around.

Perrin pressed her palm to her chest until her heartbeat slowed. She went back to class and pretended to do algebra. On the screen, the car rotated in a slow, hungry circle, and in her mind, Eric's voice turned it into a promise: *You do this, and you belong to me.*

The rest of the afternoon crawled.

Between periods, Mangelu Dinkh shoulder-checked Perrin hard enough to jolt her spine. "Saw your little street-ballet this morning, Roberts," she said. "You trying to be roadkill for views?"

Perrin swallowed the retort that would have made things worse. Keri pulled her away. "Don't feed trolls before midterms."

"Also after midterms," Taloni said. "And during."

Rosha was quiet, gaze flicking between Perrin and the corners of the hall like she expected something to materialize out of the air. Twice she opened her mouth, then shut it. Finally she said, "If you feel wrong, text me. Even if it's stupid."

"I'm fine," Perrin lied.

At the final bell, the hall exploded with bodies. Backpacks slammed lockers, teachers barked last-minute homework reminders, the intercom coughed static. Perrin moved with the river until she wasn't moving with it anymore. She slipped out of the current and let herself be drawn toward the math wing like iron filings to a magnet.

The classroom door was propped open. Inside, a knot of kids surrounded Mr. Gasker's desk, peppering him with questions. He loved an audience almost as much as he loved torque. That helped.

Perrin crossed the threshold and stood at the edges of the cluster. The keys lay on the desk—fob, metal tag stamped with a barcode, the kind of heavy, milled-aluminum thing designed to feel like a weapon in the hand.

"Is the paint reactive?" someone asked.

"Caviar metallic," Gasker said, delighted. "If you breathe on it, an angel loses its wings."

Laughter. Shoulders jostled. The knot shifted, squeezing Gasker's view to the left.

Perrin didn't think. She didn't weigh consequences. She moved when the invisible string tugged.

Her fingers closed around the fob. It was warm, like someone had just held it—even though no one had. The metal pressed crescents into her damp palm.

She slipped it into her hoodie pocket and stepped back, pulse thundering. No one noticed. Or if they did, their brains slid around the sight like oil on glass.

She walked out. Left. Down the hall. Out the front doors.

The parking lot baked in late-day light. Heat warped the air above the blacktop, but the prototype looked cool, like a chunk of night had decided to be a car. The iridescent paint threw green into blue, blue into black, until the body seemed to flex.

He stood by the driver's door. Of course he did. His smile was small, satisfied.

Perrin stopped a few yards away, chest tight, joy and terror hot in her throat. This is it, she told herself. This is the moment. You bring him the keys, he takes your hand, and this stupid ordinary life evaporates like sprinkler water on asphalt.

She pulled the fob from her pocket and held it out. He took it, his fingers brushing her knuckles, and the touch sent that familiar shiver snapping up her wrist.

"Good girl," he said. Not unkind. Not kind.

He turned away. She darted around to the passenger side, fingers already wrapped around the handle, waiting for the click of the lock.

Inside the school, a shout went up—distant, muffled. Mr. Gasker had discovered something was missing.

Perrin didn't hear. She was busy smiling at the tinted glass, at her warped reflection, at a future she'd been promised with a look.

The locks didn't click.

She blinked. Tried the handle. Nothing.

"Eric?" she said, soft now, then louder. "Eric, let me in."

He slid into the driver's seat and closed the door with a sealed, expensive thump. The cabin lights glowed for a heartbeat, then went out, his face transformed into a pale mask behind the glass.

"Please," she said, knocking. "You said—"

He rolled the window down two inches. Air conditioning spilled out, the scent of new leather and something cold.

His mouth shaped words she couldn't hear. His fingers traced a little twist in the air, like turning an invisible key.

The warm fog inside her skull lifted like a curtain in a breeze.

Confusion hit first. Then horror. Then the blood-hot flush of realizing she wasn't the only one on this side of the glass.

Behind her, students were gathering, phones out, a murmur being born.

"Eric," she tried again, voice cracking, "please—"

He smiled without teeth and rolled the window up. The engine woke, a deep mechanical animal. He dropped the car into gear.

"Eric!" She pounded the glass.

The car eased forward, nosed through the watching bodies, and then, with a sharp bark of acceleration, shot toward the exit lane.

Perrin stumbled after it, useless. Laughter chased her. Someone whooped. Someone else said, "Oh my, get this— get this."

She and the car reached the curb at the same time: him gliding onto the street, her breathless and blinking, hand still pressed to the passenger window that wasn't there anymore.

A voice detonated behind her. "WHERE ARE MY

KEYS?"

Mr. Gasker.

Dozens of fingers swung toward Perrin like weather vanes.

Her mouth opened. Nothing came out. Then everything did.

"That boy used me," she rasped, and only then realized it wasn't an excuse. It was the truth.

The circle around Perrin tightened like a noose.

Kids shoved their phones high, recording from every angle. Mr. Gasker pushed through them, face red, eyes wide, blazer flapping like he was about to dive into a war zone.

"Miss Roberts," he thundered, "give me my keys."

"They're gone," Perrin croaked. "He—he took them."

"Who?" His voice cracked. He grabbed her wrists before she could flinch. "Who?"

"Eric," she whispered, too soft. Then louder: "The boy. The tall one with the—he was just here—"

"Which Eric?" someone snorted. "Half the school's named Eric."

"Was he even a student?" another kid said, gleeful.

"Looked too old to be a student," someone else chimed in. "Like, grad student old. Or cult leader old."

"That's not funny," Mr. Gasker snapped. He turned on Perrin again. "Keys. Where are my keys."

"I gave them to him," Perrin admitted. The words tasted like rust. "He asked and I—I—"

The crowd howled. Some jeered, some clapped. One girl yelled, "Obedient girlfriend goals!"

Gasker's nostrils flared. "Principal's office. Now."

Hands shoved her backpack into hers. She stumbled, half-walked, half-dragged herself back toward the building. The laughter followed, sticky as gum on her shoes.

Rosha's face appeared in the crowd, pale and set. She didn't say anything, but her gaze tracked Perrin all the way up the steps like a tether.

The principal's office smelled of copy paper and lemon cleaner. The secretary barely looked up before calling into the inner office: "She's here."

Mr. Hollis was a square man in a square chair, with a haircut that looked like it had been measured with a level. He steepled his fingers when Perrin sat down. Beside him, Mr. Gasker paced, muttering "unbelievable" under his breath.

"Miss Roberts," Hollis said, voice flat as a ruler, "would you like to explain why you removed property from a faculty member's desk and handed it to an unauthorized person?"

Perrin twisted her fingers together. "I don't— I mean, yes, but—" Her tongue knotted. "He asked. I didn't think. I just—"

"Who is he?" Hollis asked.

She shook her head. "Eric."

"Eric who?"

"I don't know."

"You don't know?" Hollis's brows lifted. "You're telling me you gave away the keys to a prototype vehicle, one parked on my campus, to a stranger you cannot identify?"

Her throat locked. The word yes hovered like a guillotine blade. She nodded.

Hollis pinched the bridge of his nose. "Miss Roberts, do you realize the liability this creates? That car is worth more than this entire campus. Space Tech Corporation will—"

"Expel her!" Gasker barked. "Make an example. She's a walking disaster."

Perrin flinched.

Hollis held up a hand. "Calm down, Philip." His eyes stayed on Perrin. "You'll wait here until security finishes reviewing the footage. If this Eric person appears on camera, we'll pursue him. If not—" He let the silence stretch. "Well. Let's hope he appears."

The secretary ushered her into a side room—more storage closet than waiting area, stacked with outdated textbooks and the sour scent of dust. A single plastic chair. No window.

She sat. Time slowed. Her pulse beat in her fingertips.

You'll get Mr. Gasker's keys. Bring them to me.

The command still echoed. But the fog was gone. She

could see how wrong it had been, how her will had folded like paper. Shame pressed into her ribs.

The door cracked open. Rosha slipped inside, face flushed from running. She shut it behind her before the secretary noticed.

"Perrin," she whispered. "What happened?"

Perrin's mouth trembled. "I don't know. He asked. And I—like—my brain—"

Rosha crouched in front of her, dark braid swinging. "Listen to me. This is not your fault."

"I stole a car."

"You didn't." Rosha's voice was fierce. "He made you. I saw it in your eyes. You weren't there. Not the real you."

Tears threatened. Perrin pressed her fists against them. "Everyone thinks I did it on purpose."

"Let them think." Rosha's grip landed on her hands, steady and warm. "I'll find out who he is."

"How?" Perrin's voice cracked.

"My grandfather taught me to watch for patterns. Shadows move before men do. I saw his shadow on the wall this morning before he appeared." Her gaze sharpened. "He doesn't belong here. That means he leaves traces. I'll follow."

Before Perrin could answer, the door swung wider. The secretary's disapproving face appeared. "No visitors."

Rosha rose smoothly, squeezed Perrin's shoulder, and left without argument. But her eyes promised: I'm not letting this go.

By the time security was finished, the sun had started to slide. Perrin's phone buzzed with missed texts—Keri asking if she was expelled yet, Taloni sending memes, Rosha's silence louder than words.

Hollis called her back in. He didn't look happy. Gasker looked murderous.

"The footage is inconclusive," Hollis said, clipped. "A male figure is visible, but the resolution is poor. No clear face. No record of him entering the parking lot. We will pass this along to law enforcement."

"So she walks?" Gasker snapped. "Just like that?"

"She's suspended pending investigation," Hollis said, fixing Perrin with a look that felt like the nail in a coffin. "Effective immediately."

Perrin's stomach hollowed. Suspended. Not expelled. Yet. But close enough to taste.

Hollis leaned forward. "You will go home. You will not return to school until we contact your mother. Do you understand?"

"Yes," she whispered.

Gasker slammed a fist into his palm. "Space Tech Corporation is going to crucify us."

Hollis's sigh was long. "We'll deal with Space Tech Corp. For now—Miss Roberts, go."

The secretary escorted her out like a criminal.

Students still loitered by the office, whispering, phones buzzing. The words "car thief" stuck to her skin like stickers.

Outside, the air burned with desert heat, but she felt cold. Her house wasn't far. She didn't want to go there. Not yet.

"Perrin." Rosha's voice was soft but urgent. She appeared from behind the library wall, shadow long in the late sun. "Come."

Perrin hesitated. Then followed.

They ended up behind the bleachers, where the ground was patchy with gravel and weeds. It was quiet, except for the distant hum of cicadas.

"Tell me everything he said," Rosha urged.

Perrin repeated it. The words, the cadence, the way the fog had rolled in and rolled out. She didn't even realize she was shaking until Rosha caught her wrist.

"It was a command," Rosha said firmly. "Not a request. He pulled you under."

Perrin shivered. "So what do I do? If he can just—make me?"

"You don't face him alone," Rosha said. Her jaw tightened. "And you don't let shame trick you into silence. That's what he's counting on."

Perrin swallowed. "Do you believe me?"

"Yes," Rosha said, like it wasn't even a question.

A knot in Perrin's chest loosened. Not much, but enough.

Rosha glanced at the horizon, where the light bled gold into purple. "Go home. I'll look. He's not done. And neither am I."

Perrin wanted to argue, but she was too tired. She let Rosha's certainty carry her for now.

She walked home under the bruised sky, every step heavier.

Perrin trudged the last block home with her head ducked low, as if hiding from the whole neighborhood. Her sneakers slapped the sidewalk in short, angry strides, but no matter how fast she walked, she couldn't outrun the sting of laughter still echoing in her ears. The images replayed in her mind like a cruel loop: Eric, in Mr. Gasker's car pulling away, her palms slapping at the passenger-side glass, the other kids recording, jeering, chanting her name like it was a punchline.

By the time her house came into view, her stomach had tied itself into a sailor's knot. The porch light was already on, though it wasn't anywhere near dark. That meant one thing: her mother was called home from and was waiting.

The screen door creaked open before she even reached the steps.

"Inside." Pandra's voice was sharp as flint.

Perrin hesitated, half-hoping Grandma Roberts might

be the one to greet her. But no, it was her mother standing there, arms folded, her black work jacket still on, a storm cloud in human form.

Perrin dragged herself inside. The cool air of the living room didn't soothe her; it only made her shiver.

"Keys," Pandra snapped.

"I—"

"Now."

Perrin dug into her pocket and handed over the key ring that had been weighing her down all afternoon. She hadn't realized until this moment how much she'd hoped Eric would explain, would turn it into some grand romantic adventure instead of a public execution.

Pandra pocketed the keys. "Do you have any idea what you've done?"

"Yes! I mean, no! It wasn't me, Mom, he made me do it —"

Her words came out tangled, desperate, but Pandra cut her off with a raised hand.

"I don't want excuses. You stole a teacher's car. That's not something you just bounce back from with a sorry and a shrug."

"I didn't steal it!" Perrin's voice cracked. "He—Eric—he hypnotized me or something. I swear! He—he told me to, and I just... I don't even know how, but I couldn't say no —"

"You think I'm going to swallow that?" Pandra's jaw flexed. "You think the school board will swallow that?"

Perrin's cheeks burned hot. She wished more than anything she had the video to prove it — the way his eyes seemed to draw her in like black holes, the way the command dropped into her head like someone else's thought. But of course she hadn't checked before sending it to Social Media and of course it was gone now, drowned out by the clips everyone else posted of her humiliating plea at the car door.

Her mother turned toward the kitchen, voice clipped. "Sit. Don't move."

Perrin dropped into a chair, arms crossed, every cell in her body trembling with a mix of anger and panic.

A few minutes later, a knock rattled the front door.

The officer was brief — ankle bracelet, curfew conditions, stern warnings about consequences. Perrin sat stone-faced as the woman fastened the sleek black band around her ankle, its small green light blinking like an accusation. The whole time, Pandra stood by with her arms folded tight, lips pressed into a line.

When the officer left, silence crashed down heavier than before.

"You're grounded for thirty days," Pandra said finally. "No phone. No friends. No wandering off. You do your school work, you stay home, you breathe under my roof. That's it."

"That's not fair!" Perrin burst out, her chair scraping back. "You don't believe me! None of you ever believe me!"

"You've given me no reason to."

The words cut deeper than Perrin expected. She flinched, then shoved her chair in and stormed toward the hallway.

"Perrin."

Her mother's voice had softened, but she didn't look back.

Grandma Roberts intercepted her instead. She was sitting in her armchair like she had been waiting all along, knitting needles idle in her lap. Her silver hair caught the glow from the lamp beside her, her face calm where Pandra's was carved from stone.

"Come here, sweetheart."

Perrin slumped into the arm of the chair, the anger draining out as quickly as it had boiled up.

"You made a mistake," Grandma said gently. "But don't let one mistake convince you that's all you are."

"I didn't even make it!" Perrin wailed. "It was him. I swear it was him. I didn't want to do it. I thought—" Her throat closed up, the words too humiliating to finish. *I thought he loved me.*

Grandma rested a warm hand over Perrin's. "Your father loved you fiercely, before..." She trailed off, eyes flicking toward Pandra in the kitchen, and the silence stretched like a curtain drawn across secrets.

"Before what?" Perrin asked, her heart kicking up. "What are you saying?"

Grandma only squeezed her hand and let go. "Before he vanished."

"What exactly happened to him?"

Perrin's grandmother motioned for the door to be shut. Perrin closed it quietly.

"It was when you were only nine months old. Your mother heard a noise and woke your father to go investigate it. He stumbled out the front door in his pajamas and slippers. Your mother heard a scuffle on the side of the house. She ran out and saw no one. Just one of your father's slippers on the front sidewalk." Grandma Grace's eyes misted up. Perrin remembered that her father was Grace's son.

"Thanks for telling me, Grandma," said Perrin. Her grandmother nodded while trying to wipe her tears away."

Later, in her bedroom, Perrin lay flat on her back, staring at the green blink of the ankle bracelet. It mocked her with every pulse. *Grounded. Trapped. Labeled.*

Through her window she saw the street below, lit by porch lamps and the soft hum of a late summer night. Two houses down, one of her classmates ran into her father's arms, laughing as he swung her up off her feet. Another dad hoisted his daughter's science fair project out of the car, balancing it like treasure. Perrin's chest ached watching them.

Her dad should've been there. He should've been the one standing in the yard, proud, protective, not vanishing like smoke years ago, leaving her with nothing but questions and whispers.

A floorboard creaked. Grandma Roberts stepped into the room, leaning on her cane, eyes softer than ever.

Perrin turned her face away, embarrassed.

Grandma crossed to the window and stood looking out at the night for a long moment. Then she said quietly, almost to herself, "That thing won't keep you safe, Perrin. It's what's under your feet you need to be careful of."

Perrin sat up, startled. "What does that mean?"

But Grandma only smiled faintly and patted her shoulder. "Sleep, sweetheart. You'll need your strength."

Then she was gone, leaving Perrin staring after her, the ankle bracelet pulsing in the dark, and a strange new fear gnawing under her skin.

The ankle bracelet wasn't heavy, but it felt like a shackle. Every time Perrin moved, the plastic cuff rubbed against her skin, digging in just enough to remind her that she was under lock and key. She sat on the edge of her bed, chin in her hands, staring at the green light blinking faintly in the dim room. A stupid little dot that said: *You're trapped. You're not trusted. You're a prisoner in your own house.*

Downstairs, voices carried through the old air vents. Her mother's voice was clipped, sharp enough to slice through the walls. "She *stole* a car, Grace! Do you understand that? A car worth more than this entire block! What am I supposed to do—just pretend it was a prank?"

Her grandmother's voice, lower but firm, rumbled back. "You're overreacting, Pandra. She's a girl, not a hardened criminal."

"She could've ruined *everything*." A pause, then Pandra again, lower now, almost a growl. "If she keeps this up, maybe I should tell her the truth. Scare her straight."

Perrin leaned closer to the vent, heart thudding. *The truth about what?*

"You will *not* tell her yet," Grandma Roberts snapped. "Fear won't save her—it'll only push her closer to the danger."

The pause that followed was worse than the words.

Perrin pressed her ear to the wall until the paint chilled her skin. She wanted to know—needed to know—but the boards creaked under her shifting weight. Instantly, the voices cut off.

Silence.

She stayed frozen, hardly breathing, until her legs ached. But neither voice came back. They were talking about her, yes—but also about something else. Something they didn't trust her with.

With a muttered curse, Perrin pushed back from the wall and dropped onto her bed. The mattress groaned in sympathy. She pulled her blanket over her legs, glaring down at the stupid blinking bracelet. Its green light pulsed in the shadows, steady, patient, relentless.

She whispered into the dark, barely moving her lips. "Why does everyone know something about me... except me?"

The words hung in the quiet like smoke.

And then—so faint she thought she imagined it—she felt it: a vibration through the floorboards. A tremor, almost like the earth beneath her room had shivered.

She sucked in a sharp breath and sat up, holding still. The house gave no further sound, only the steady tick of the wall clock.

But Perrin couldn't shake the thought that the ground itself had just whispered back to her.

CHAPTER 3: THE SUPERSTITION MISSION

Breakfast tried to be normal and failed.

Perrin sat at the end of the table where the sun cut a rectangle across the placemat and turned the dust in the air into glitter. Her cereal was a soggy island. The ankle bracelet blinked its patient green under the table, tapping a rhythm against her skin that she could not stop noticing.

Pandra spooned instant cocoa mix into hot water and stirred it like she was punishing the mug. Her jaw worked while she checked the sugar bowl. She didn't look at Perrin when she set the mug down, didn't look when she slid a second mug to the opposite chair for Grandma Roberts, didn't look when she taped a sheet of paper to the refrigerator with a slap that said it was not a suggestion.

Grandma watched everything, hands wrapped around her mug as if warming them, eyes soft but sharp. When Perrin finally lifted her head, Grandma gave her a look that meant *breathe first, talk second.*

Pandra broke the silence. "Phone."

Perrin's spoon paused halfway to her mouth. "Seriously?"

"Phone," Pandra repeated, palm out.

It was already in Perrin's pocket. She had slept with it curled in her palm like a talisman, checking it in the middle of the night as if some good news would arrive to dissolve yesterday. She unlocked it with her thumb, stared once at the home screen—a grid of tiny doors to rooms she wasn't allowed to enter anymore—and set it in Pandra's hand.

Pandra didn't gloat. She dropped the phone into a ceramic bowl on the counter with the keys and spare change. The clink sounded final in a way the ankle bracelet hadn't.

"I need it for school," Perrin said.

"You can use the house laptop at the table," Pandra said. "In plainsight."

"What about my friends?"

"Friends can knock on the door," Pandra said. "If they're friends."

"That's—" Perrin swallowed the last word. Unfair had been thrown around too much already and bounced off everything.

From the street came the thrum of a lawnmower. Voices carried through the open kitchen window: two moms out front with strollers, pausing to gossip. One of them said, low and scandalized, "—the video—at the car —begging—" and the other made the little sympathetic cluck people make when they're thrilled something isn't happening to them.

Perrin stared at her cereal until the cornflakes turned to paste. Somewhere in the neighborhood a kid imitated her voice, "Eric, let me in!" and a chorus of laughter followed, that high-pitched, merciless kind that only kids manage. Grandma's mouth thinned. Pandra's shoulders stiffened, but she didn't go to the window to shut it. She let the sounds exist, like weather.

When Pandra finally sat across from Perrin, she didn't touch her cocoa. "Here's what's happening," she said, voice even. "You are on house arrest for thirty days. You do not step past the property line without me or Grandma. No sleepovers. No parties. No 'quick walks.' If I'm at work, you're with your grandmother. If I say no, it's no. If you argue with me about no, it's still no."

"I got it," Perrin muttered.

"I'm not finished." Pandra nodded toward the refrigerator. "Read it."

Perrin pushed back from the table and went to the paper. The list was handwritten in block letters, too neat to be angry writing, which somehow made it worse.

HOUSE RULES — PERRIN

1. **Check in** every two hours while awake.

2. **Chores:** diswasher, trash, livingroom vacuum M/W/F.

3. **Homework** at kitchen table 4-6 pm (no headphones).

4. **No Social Media.** (No exceptions. Don't test me.)

5. **No guests** without clearance.

6. **No leaving property** (bracelet geofence = 25 ft past mailbox).

7. **Lights out** by 10 p.m. Phone stays in bowl.

At the bottom, in smaller letters: **We will talk when you're honest.—Mom**

Honest. Like she'd chosen to be dishonest.

Grandma set a legal pad and a pen beside Perrin's bowl. "Write what you can't say," she murmured.

Perrin stared at the pad. The first instinct rose hot and fast: Nope. Not playing this therapy game. But her fingers closed on the pen anyway, like they hadn't got the memo from her pride.

The ankle bracelet ticked against the chair rung. It wasn't loud. The slightest tap, plastic on wood. Her skin itched underneath it, and she scratched without thinking. Pandra's eyes snapped to her hand.

"Don't pick at it," she said. Not harsh. Warning.

"I'm not—" Perrin pulled her nails away. Static crawled up her calf like the thing had a charge. "It itches."

"It's supposed to remind you," Pandra said. "Let it."

Grandma's gaze softened. "Let it remind you you're alive, not that you're trapped."

Pandra breathed in through her nose and tried again. "Look. I'm angry. That's not a secret. But I'm also... I'm scared. This could have gone so much worse."

"I know," Perrin said, because that was the safest answer.

"What I'm asking from you is simple," Pandra continued. "For one month, do what you're told. No stunts. No experiments. No videos. We'll figure the rest out when you're not an internet spectacle and I'm not waiting for a call from a lawyer."

"I said I know," Perrin said. The words came out flatter than she meant.

Grandma cleared her throat. "Eat."

Perrin lifted her spoon and forced the cereal down, each bite a gray, milky effort. She could feel the two women on either side of her like bookends—one made of granite, the other of old oak—their entire history withher pressing in from both sides.

When breakfast broke up, Pandra took the mug and the bowl to the sink, rinsed them, and set them in the dishwasher with unnecessary precision. She glanced at the time on the microwave. "Homework at four," she said, as if the clock needed to hear it.

"Yes, ma'am."

"And Perrin?" Pandra paused, hand still on the dishwasher handle. When she looked back, some of the steel had leaked out of her eyes, and what was left was just tired. "You are not stupid."

Perrin flinched like the word itself had teeth. "I didn't say—"

"You don't have to say," Pandra said. "It sits on you when you think I'm not looking."

She left before Perrin could answer. Grandma stood, gathered the pad and pen, and then, as if changing her mind, left them where they were. "If the phone is a door that opens to noise," she said, "this is a door that opens to you." She tapped the paper. "Use it, or don't. But don't forget the door exists."

The front window thumped. A basketball bounced off the glass and rolled across the porch. A voice shouted, "Sorry!"—a boy from down the block who never looked sorry when he said it. His friend laughed, "Dude, you see the clip? She—"

Grandma closed the window with a firm snap and drew the curtains halfway, not enough to make the house a cave, just enough to make the world fuzzier.

Perrin stayed at the table after they left the room. The house felt different without her phone humming in the bowl of her palm—quieter and louder at the same time.

The refrigerator ticked as it cycled. Somewhere a dryer turned and turned. The ankle bracelet blinked, blinked, blinked, like a slow heartbeat separate from her own.

She clicked the pen. Wrote nothing. Clicked it again.

On the pad, she finally printed: **DAY 1** Under it, she drew a box and wrote **don't cry** next to it, then checked the box immediately and snorted despite herself.

She added another box: **things I didn't choose**
Under that:

1) **Eric.**
2) **the internet.**
3) **being a joke.**
4) **this...** and she arrowed the pen down to her drawing of her leg with the ankle bracelet.

From the hallway, Pandra called, "Trash," like she was reminding Perrin how to be a person. Perrin stood, shouldered the bag, and took it out to the bin on the side of the house, careful not to step past the gravel seam that Grandma had always called the property line.

The sun had already cleared the roofline and turned the driveway into a griddle. Across the street, Mrs. Moreno watered the ocotillo with a hose set to mist and pretended not to glance over. Her daughter, a grade below Perrin, stood beside her in glitter slides, texting with her head bent, thumbs fast. When she looked up, she flinched like Perrin had shouted, then pasted on a smile and waved a too-fast wave that meant *I saw, everyone saw.*

"Morning," Perrin managed.

"Morning, mija," Mrs. Moreno said, too bright. "Hot one today."

"Yeah."

Back inside, Perrin washed her hands at the kitchen sink. Grandma had left a dish towel folded into a perfect square, the kind of little order that made chaos feel negotiable. Perrin dried her hands on it and set it back the same way. It felt like betrayal to crumple it.

She sat at the table at four because she'd been told to. Pandra set the house laptop in front of her and logged in, then angled the screen so it reflected the room more than Perrin's face. "Homework," she said, not leaning on the word, just setting it down between them like a load neither of them wanted.

Perrin opened the school portal and stared at assignments that felt pulled from another person's life. Math. English. Biology. Words that used to be scaffolding now looked like salt lines on a wall after a flood.

The ankle bracelet itched again. She dug the capped pen under the edge to scratch, caught herself, and yanked it back out like she'd put a fork in an outlet.

"Don't test the alarm," Pandra said without looking up from the counter where she was sorting mail.

"I wasn't."

"Mhm."

At some point, Grandma slipped a small square of

chocolate beside the laptop without a word, like a kindness dropped into a donation jar. Perrin ate it slowly, letting it melt, refusing to cry again because she'd already checked that box.

By six, the house smelled like onions and cumin. Pandra cooked like she fought—decisive, efficient, leaving nothing half-done. Grandma chopped cilantro with a knife that had been sharpened so many times it had become a different blade. At dinner there was conversation about nothing: the neighbor's cat, the HOA newsletter, the way the heat would break in a month if the rains were kind. No one mentioned Eric. No one said hypnotized. No one said *I believe you*.

When the dishes were finished and the sun finally slid low enough to make the living room glow, Grandma took the legal pad from the table, read nothing, and put it back exactly where Perrin had left it.

"Day one," she said with a small nod, like a coach sending a runner to the next lap.

Perrin went to her room at ten because the list said so. She set her hands on the windowsill and stared out into the night. The street had reset itself into quiet. Somewhere, a radio played a slow song. Somewhere else, a coyote yipped, thin as thread. The ankle bracelet blinked in the dark. She clicked the pen once and set it down.

Day one didn't feel like surviving. It felt like learning how to breathe with a hand over her mouth.

She did it anyway.

Day Two tasted like cardboard.

Perrin rinsed her cereal bowl, set it carefully in the dishwasher, and checked the refrigerator list because checking it felt like doing something. The ankle bracelet blinked without hurry. She could feel its circle even when she wasn't looking—skin there a shade lighter, like a finger where a ring never comes off.

Outside, the neighborhood moved on without her. A garage door yawned. Someone revved a motorcycle. A jogger in a neon shirt sailed past the window, ponytail steady, not a prisoner to anything but her own lungs.

Grandma slid a fresh page of the legal pad in front of Perrin. *Write what you can't say*, the first page still urged in Grandma's looping hand.

Perrin wrote, **I didn't choose any of this**, then crossed it out so hard the paper scarred.

At Rosha's house, her notes didn't look like a detective's; they looked like a smart girl trying not to talk herself out of what she knew.

She wrote **ERIC** at the top of a page and drew a box around it.

Underneath: **stairs video — hand gesture / voice cadence**.

Then: **shadow led, body followed**. She circled that three times.

On her laptop, she logged into the school portal and searched the student directory. **Shiver, Eric** yielded nothing. **Shivers**: three results—none a transfer, none a senior with gray eyes and a smile like he wore it to see what it would do to you. Some girl lamented that Eric's name was called in class and he wasn't there, but she mentioned his last name. That's how Rosha got it.

She pulled up the clip of the prototype car leaving— the one someone had posted from the far edge of the lot. She freeze-framed over and over, looking for what didn't belong. The crowd's shadows ran north-west, long and smudged. The boy's? It was there, yes—but it seemed to hesitate where the others were decisive, like a slick of oil trying to remember how to be water.

Rosha chewed the end of her pencil. "You're not a god," she murmured to the screen, "you're a hunger."

She wrote it down.

Then she closed the laptop, put on her sneakers, and went back to the parking lot after dinner when no one would bother a girl pretending she'd lost a bracelet. Near the space where the prototype had idled, the sun had baked the asphalt hard, but in the dust strip between spaces she found narrow prints. Not student shoes—too little rubber pattern, almost no heel flower. She crouched, palms on her knees, and felt ridiculous and right at the same time.

Across the lot, a security light buzzed. Rosha stood and made herself a quiet promise: **Protect Perrin quietly.** No speeches that could be laughed off. No texts that could be screen shotted. She would carry the weird truth like an ember in her pocket until the moment it was needed.

Week One: Perrin did the chores, her schoolwork, all with no phone. The house laptop tracked every keypress like it wanted to file a report. Perrin did the dishes and the trash and the vacuuming on M/W/F, because the list said so and because sometimes obeying made the chaos stop humming.

She wrote three unsent letters to her dad on Grandma's pad.

> *Dear Dad, today I learned a car can look like a shark. You would have told me not to chase sharks.*

> *Dear Dad, if you're alive, are you a coward for not coming back or a hero for staying gone?*

> *Dear Dad, I'm sorry I'm a joke. I don't know how to be anything else yet.*

She never showed them to anyone. She tore two out and hid them in a book; she left the third on the pad and pretended it was someone else's handwriting.

Week Two: heat rose off the street like something living. A neighbor rang the bell to ask if Pandra had seen the HOA email about "improper refuse bin storage" and somehow worked in, "Kids are cruel on the internet these days, aren't they?" Perrin stood in the hall and tried to breathe without sounding like she was listening.

Perrin loosened by degrees, not by speeches. She started leaving the kitchen light on for Pandra when she was late home from work, a small square of brightness that said *I knew you were coming through this door.* Twice, her mother almost said something that sounded like a secret, starting with "When I was your age—" and "There's a reason I—" and both times she closed the cupboard harder than necessary and said, "Hand me the oregano."

Week Three: Perrin watched other girls with their dads from the upstairs window without meaning to. The moments found her. A messy bun, a girl on tiptoe to put her arms around her father's neck. A father setting down a toolbox to fix a bike chain. It made her angry for a while, sharp, sparking. Then the anger cooled into something harder and quieter. *I won't be stupid again;* she wrote on the pad and drew a box to check later.

A note came in the mailbox without a stamp. **I believe you. Don't answer. Just know. —R** Perrin hid it between the pages of *The Illustrated Encyclopedia of Mammals* because no one had opened that book in her lifetime.

Week Four: the ankle bracelet stopped feeling like a clamp and started feeling like a border marker she could lean on. She stood in the yard with Grandma one evening, toes on the gravel seam that meant **25 feet past the mailbox** was off limits. The bracelet hummed once when she leaned too far, a tiny warning, and she rocked back. Grandma didn't say *good girl* or *careful*; she held out a piece of watermelon and said, "Eat before the ants figure out you've got it and swarm you."

Sometimes at night the house gave a sound that wasn't plumbing or the icemaker. Perrin told herself it was settling. She did not write that down.

Removal Day was brighter than it deserved to be.

The officer wore sunglasses and looked like she'd been told not to be friendly. The key slid into the cuff, turned, and the small green light blinked twice and went dark. The band opened with a whisper. Perrin didn't mean to exhale loudly, but her leg felt suddenly feather-light and wrong, like a cast coming off a broken bone.

"You're not free and clear," the officer said. "Call comes in, I come back. Thin ice. You understand?"

"Yes," Perrin said. Her skin where the bracelet had been pale and tender. She resisted the urge to rub it.

Pandra signed the last paper and handed the clipboard back. Her phone buzzed as if it had been waiting for that exact second. She glanced at the screen, and everything in her face went still.

"Pandra?" Grandma said.

"Excuse me." Pandra moved two steps away and answered. "Roberts." A beat. "Understood." Another beat. "Coordinates?" She wrote on the back of an envelope, repeating the numbers. "We're on our way."

When she hung up, she was already moving. "Pack water. Boots. Hat," she told Perrin. "Now."

"What—?"

"Now."

Grandma didn't ask. She went to the hall closet, took down the small olive drab pack Pandra kept there for emergencies that "never happen," and began stuffing it with what emergencies always needed: gauze, iodine, a roll of tape, a coil of cord, a folded foil blanket. She tucked a blue kerchief into the top of the pack and then changed her mind, pulled it out, and pressed it into Perrin's hand.

"For sweat," Grandma said loudly enough for the officer still at the door to hear, and then, softer: "For luck."

Perrin tied it to her belt loop with fingers that wouldn't behave. "Where are we going?"

"East," Pandra said, checking the pantry for the good water bottles. "You're with me."

"I thought I wasn't allowed to leave the property."

"That was before the call."

"What call?"

Pandra stopped long enough to look Perrin in the eyes. There was steel there, yes, but also something like sorrow that had misplaced its map. "Someone I work with went missing. Same area I told you about."

"The Superstitions," Perrin said. Her mouth went dry. "The mines."

"Boots," Pandra repeated pointing at Perrin's feet.

In her room, Perrin yanked on her high-tops, the ones with scuffed toes and decent tread. She grabbed her hat from the hook—wide brim, ugly, perfect—and a hoodie she could tie around her waist in case the desert decided to pretend it had evenings. She jammed a granola bar into her pocket because survival looked like that on TV.

When she clattered back down the hall, Pandra was at the garage door with her keys already in hand. The officer had gone. Grandma stood in the kitchen doorway with her arms folded, not blocking, just witnessing.

"Pay attention," Grandma said, the same way she had said **eat** and **sleep**—not a suggestion, not a threat, a duty.

Perrin nodded without knowing what she was agreeing to.

They were halfway down the block before Pandra spoke again. "No photos," she said.

Perrin opened her mouth to point out the obvious— *you took my phone*—and closed it again. The truck's AC coughed to life and then settled into a steady cool that smelled faintly of dust and old cocoa. The neighborhood slipped away behind them: the cookie-cutter roofs, the low cacti, the kids on scooters who would someday have their own humiliations and would pretend not to remember hers.

The freeway east unspooled like a ribbon. Heat shimmered above the lanes. In the distance, the Superstition Mountains rose out of the desert like knuckles punched up through a table.

Perrin watched them come closer and felt the strangest double pull—fear, yes, but something else too, like standing at the edge of a pool and remembering you used to know how to swim.

She folded Grandma's blue kerchief in her lap until the creases lined up neat. Then she unfolded it and did it again.

The truck's AC coughed like it was trying too hard against the desert heat. Perrin slumped into the passenger seat, arms folded, ankle still sore from where the bracelet had rubbed. Pandra kept her eyes on the road, jaw set as tight as the steering wheel in her grip.

"So what are you, then?" Perrin finally muttered. "CIA? Monster hunter? Vampire exterminator?" She gave a short laugh, hoping to crack the wall.

Pandra didn't even look at her. "You'll see soon enough."

Not the comeback Perrin wanted. Her smirk slid away, leaving silence in its place. Outside, the highway stretched like a black ribbon into wavering heat. The red cliffs on the horizon rose like broken knuckles punching through the desert floor.

Perrin chewed her lip, restless. "Was Dad in trouble? Is that why—"

"Seatbelt," Pandra cut in, sharp.

Perrin clicked it into place, heat flaring in her cheeks. She turned to the window, watching mesquite trees whip past, brittle and dry.

After a while, Pandra's voice softened, but not much. "If I tell you to get behind me, you do it. No questions. No photos. Not one."

It landed more like a commandment than advice. Perrin nodded, though she wasn't sure her mother saw it.

Pandra reached behind the truck seat with one hand, fishing out a bundle wrapped in oilcloth. She checked it, quick but careful, then positioned it across her lap. For an instant Perrin caught the gleam of obsidian teeth — jagged, ancient, and sharp.

Her throat went dry. "That's... a sword?"

Pandra's eyes stayed on the road. "A teacher."

The word hung there, heavy and strange. Perrin slumped back, heart thudding against her ribs. Whatever this trip was, it wasn't a ghost-tour.

The truck rattled onto a washboard road, dust billowing in its wake. Redrock rose in jagged towers ahead, like broken knuckles clawing at the sky. Pandra guided the wheel with one hand, the other resting protectively on the wrapped bundle on her lap.

They pulled into a dirt turnout; little more than a scar scraped into the desert edge. Two figures waited at the trailhead, already haloed in heat shimmer.

One was lean and angular, sunburnt skin pulled tight over sharp cheekbones. He leaned against a sandstone boulder, arms folded, a long bowie-style blade strapped across his thigh.

"That's Cutter on the left against that boulder," said Pandra. Cutter barely flicked his eyes toward the truck as it rolled in.

Beside him stood a woman Perrin guessed was closer to Pandra's age. She had straight dark hair tied back, a coil of rope looped at her hip, and a knife of obsidian-black stone catching the sun like it wanted blood.

"The other is Anita," Pandar added. Anita Grayhawk

---

nodded once as they climbed out, her expression steady, reserved.

Pandra's voice cut the silence first. "Report."

Cutter's reply was a single word, flat as dry stone: "Nothing."

Anita added, "Tracks where he should've been. No return. No signal." She flicked her gaze at Perrin just long enough to note her presence, then back to Pandra.

Perrin folded her arms, heat biting her cheeks, and muttered, "Nice to meet you too."

The three adults exchanged clipped phrases—short, coded, like they'd rehearsed a language Perrin didn't speak. She caught only fragments: "hollow wind," "coordinates," "echo cut." Each word weighed too much, carried too much meaning.

When Pandra unwrapped the oil cloth, laying the macuahuitl across her forearms, Perrin finally let out the breath she'd been holding.

"That's... seriously a sword," she whispered.

Anita's eyes flicked to her. "Not a sword," she said softly. "A teacher. You don't swing it unless you're ready to learn the cost."

Cutter gave a single grunt that might have been agreement—or warning.

Perrin's stomach dropped. Whatever this was, she wasn't supposed to be here.

They moved in a slow, deliberate line, boots crunching over grit and brittle scrub. The canyon walls leaned closer, red stone rising like ancient ribs around them. Heat shimmered overhead, but down here the air carried a strange stillness—no insects buzzing, no birdcall, just the crunch of their steps.

Anita slowed first, her gaze snagging on something half-hidden in a low crevice. She reached out, fingers brushing against a small bundle of reeds bound with faded cord, the edges darkened by sun and age. A few feathers dangled from it, brittle as paper.

"What is that?" Perrin asked before she could stop herself.

Anita turned it gently, the bundle crumbling slightly in her hand. Her expression sharpened, not fear but respect. "A Native protection charm," she said quietly. "Old. And broken."

Perrin leaned closer. It didn't look like much—just reeds and feathers, like a craft project from grade school—but the hush in Anita's voice made it feel heavier.

"Broken how?" she asked.

Anita set the bundle back into the crevice, brushing the dust from her hands like she'd touched something sacred. "It's a ward," she said. "Meant to keep things out. These don't just fail."

Perrin frowned. "So...?"

Anita's mouth pressed into a flat line. "So whatever's ahead of us didn't just ignore protection—it broke it. That takes power."

Perrin felt her skin crawl. Power strong enough to tear

apart a charm that was supposed to keep monsters away.

Perrin swallowed hard. She didn't know what scared her more—that such a thing had been there at all, or that something worse had undone it.

Cutter slowed first, squatting low where the trail thinned into shale. He brushed his palm across the ground, then pointed with two fingers. "Tire tracks," he said. "But…"

Perrin squinted at the rock. The lines ran straight for ten feet, clear as pressed ink. Then they just—stopped. No dust. No scattering. Like a truck had rolled forward and dissolved.

Cutter's jaw set hard. "I don't like impossible."

They pushed on, the air thickening with heat and silence until the path bent into a low cut of red stone. A collapsed horizontal mine sagged ahead, rubble spilling down like broken teeth. To the right, a narrow slit exhaled a cool breath that prickled Perrin's arms.

"Looks like it's still breathing," Cutter muttered, eyes narrowed.

Perrin hugged herself, not sure if he meant the mine or something inside it.

"This is it," Anita said. Her voice carried the weight of a ritual. "It all leads to this collapsed horizontal mine."

Perrin edged closer, her eyes catching shapes carved into the rock. They weren't graffiti. Petroglyphs, painted in ochre and black, lines cut deep enough to last centuries.

Anita stepped forward, tracing one with her finger without touching. "Children of the Earth, keep faith below."

Another glyph—spirals bending inward. "Beware the false one from the sky who enslaves wills."

Perrin's throat tightened.

The last line curved into a symbol she didn't know, blue pigment faint but stubborn against the stone. Anita's tone softened: "Trust the Blue who fed you in the dark."

Perrin shivered. Grandma's words came back unbidden —*under your feet.*

Cutter slung his pack off one shoulder, pulling free a bundle of chem-lights. He cracked them one by one, the sharp *snap* followed by a hiss of green fire. He laid them in the slit's throat, marking a crooked trail into the dark. The glow bled across damp rock and tangled rubble, painting the passage like some underground artery.

Professional. Precise. He'd done this a hundred times before.

Perrin swallowed, throat dry. This wasn't just exploring a cave. This was entering something meant to stay closed.

Pandra shifted beside her, the Macuahuitl's obsidian edges catching a glint of green. "Stay between Anita and me," she said without looking away from the dark. Her tone carried no room for argument. "If I say down, you drop."

Perrin nodded quickly, pulse thudding in her ears. The

cold breath of the mine brushed her face like something alive, waiting.

The mine swallowed them in stages—first the sunlight thinning, then the heat falling away into damp chill. Perrin's ears rang with every drip of water, each drop echoing too long. The air had a tang that clung to her tongue, sharp and metallic, like sucking on pennies.

Her boots scuffed grit across old stone. The beam of Anita's flashlight skimmed over a frayed rope end caught between rocks, its fibers rotted and curling. A few feet further in, Cutter crouched by a dented canteen, brushing dirt off its side. Strange glyphs had been scratched into the metal—lines that bent like antlers, jagged and uneven, but purposeful.

Perrin hugged her arms, forcing herself not to ask what they meant. Every answer here seemed to cost more than it gave.

Something winked at her from the floor. She crouched before she even thought, fingers digging into cold grit until they closed around a solid weight. When she pulled it free, her breath caught—

A watch. Its cracked face was dusted with sand, hands frozen at half past seven. On the back, barely legible through wear and grime, an engraving curled into view as she rubbed with her thumb:

To Bill. All my love. —P.

The world seemed to still.

Pandra froze mid-step. She turned, eyes locking on the

watch as if she'd been stabbed. Her hand shook as she lifted it from Perrin's palm. She stared at the engraving, lips parting but no words coming out.

For the first time, Perrin heard her mother's breath break, sharp and hollow.

"Mom?" Perrin whispered. The word felt dangerous in this place.

Pandra's voice was thin, stripped raw. "Where did you find this?"

Perrin pointed to the dirt at her feet. Her chest ached without knowing why.

Anita's expression shifted, wary and grim. She looked past them into the dark. "If his things are here... he went down."

Pandra turned the watch over in her hands again and again, like she didn't trust her own eyes. The beam from Cutter's chem-light painted her face in green shadows, and Perrin swore she could see every year, every fight, every scar carved into her mother's expression at once.

"This was his," Pandra whispered. Not to anyone —more like to the rock walls, to the air that still remembered. "He never took it off. Not once."

Her thumb traced the engraving with reverence, the way someone might trace a prayer. For a heartbeat she wasn't the hard-edged woman who barked orders and carried a sword older than history. She was just... hollow.

Perrin didn't know what to do. She wanted to reach out, but her own arms felt useless. "Mom... you think he was here?"

Pandra's jaw clenched. Her voice came back, sharp as snapped glass. "No. He *is* here."

The certainty in those words frightened Perrin more than anything she'd seen since the police car. It wasn't hope—it was something harder, darker. A vow carved into stone.

Anita shifted uneasily, lowering her light. "Pandra..." she started, but stopped when Pandra's knuckles whitened around the watch.

"Don't," Pandra said flatly. "Don't tell me what this means. I already know."

For a moment the mine seemed to breathe with her fury, the walls listening, waiting. Then she slipped the watch into her pocket, shoulders locking back into armor. But Perrin had seen it—the crack in her mother's mask, the raw wound underneath.

And somehow, that frightened her more than anything waiting in the dark ahead.

The silence pressed heavy after Pandra's words, broken only by the faint drip of water deeper in the shaft. Cutter shifted his weight, the crunch of his boot too loud in the stillness.

"Whatever left this behind," he said, scanning the shadows, "it didn't walkout the front door."

The ground trembled under their feet—just a shiver at first, then a deeper rumble. Pebbles rattled down the rock wall.

"Out. Everyone out," Cutter barked, already reaching to drag Anita toward the slit.

Perrin felt the vibration rise through her ankles, into her bones. A low groan rolled from the mine's throat, as if the earth itself had drawn in a breath.

"Stay between us," Pandra snapped, stepping closer, Macuahuitl gripped white-knuckle tight. Her eyes darted from Perrin to the trembling floor. "If I say down, you drop—"

The warning cut off as the crust beneath Perrin gave way with a sharp, cracking roar.

"PERRIN!"

Her stomach lurched into her throat. She flung out her hands, fingers clawing at empty air. The ground she'd trusted turned to a collapsing funnel, rocks and grit sliding out from under her.

Pandra lunged—fast, faster than Perrin had ever seen her move. One hand clamped around Perrin's wrist, searing her skin. The Macuahuitl scraped sparks off the rock as her mother jammed it into the edge for leverage.

For a heartbeat, it held. Their eyes locked—Pandra's wide with a terror that no enemy had ever put there before.

"I've got you!" she rasped, voice tearing.

But the stone cracked under her grip, burning dust filling the air. Perrin's fingers slipped against her mother's palm, skin raw, wrist screaming.

"No!" Pandra's voice broke, shredded with something

between rage and despair.

And then Perrin was falling.

Darkness rushed up to meet her, cold wind screaming past her ears. Below, faint points of light shimmered— blue, green, shifting like something alive. Long enough to think she might die before she even touched bottom.

The last thing she heard was her mother's voice ripping itself raw into the void:

"PERRIN!"

Then only the rush of air, the plunge into black.

Cold wind swallowed her. Lights glimmered below, eerie and alive, glowing like veins in the dark. The fall stretched long enough for Perrin to know she wasn't going to stop.

The world went black.

CHAPTER 4: THE FALL AND TUSPIN

The world dropped out from under Perrin before she could scream.

Stone tore past her shoulders, then open dark yawned beneath her like a swallowed breath. Air clawed at her clothes; grit stung her cheeks; somewhere above, her mother's voice snapped in half on Perrin's name and vanished into the echoing shaft.

She braced for bone and black, for the kind of impact that rearranges a life into Before and After.

Instead, the dark flexed.

Something caught her—a mesh that gave like muscle and held like woven rope. She sank, bounced, sank again. The net wasn't rope at all, but a tangle of pale roots braided tighter than fingers, their surfaces slick with dew. Threads of fungus veined the lattice, pulsing a soft blue green that threw ghost-light across her face. Each strand trembled under her weight, then tightened, as if making up its mind about her.

Perrin lay sucked into that living hammock, lungs

heaving, ears full of her pulse. The cold pushed through her hoodie and soaked her skin with cave chill. The air smelled like wet stone, crushed aloe, and something faintly metallic, almost like coins on her tongue. Above, a pinhole of light chandeliered into dust. Far below, the dark kept going.

"Okay," she breathed, voice raw. "Okay—okay."

The net shifted in answer. Not a slide, not gravity, but an intentional lowering—sections loosening while others cinched, relieving pressure at her ribs, easing her down inch by careful inch. She couldn't see any hands. The roots themselves seemed to be deciding how not to break her.

Not possible, her brain supplied in a flat teacher voice. Not scientific. Not real.

And then another part of her, the part that had watched sprinkler water make rainbows while kids called her names, whispered back: Neither is a boy who turns your thoughts like a knob.

The roots hummed—no, that was her blood. Except as she listened, the hum separated from her heartbeat and settled into the cave itself, a low, steady vibration that Perrin felt more than heard. It ran up through the net and into her bones, like standing too close to a big speaker. The glow along the fungus brightened in a slow rhythm, as if the net were breathing.

She didn't move until the roots let her. They lowered her to a shelf of rock slick with mica and dotted in luminous caps, then unhooked themselves from her clothes with a whisper-soft shiver. The net retracted, rewinding into the walls, and the light with it dimmed to a patient shimmer.

Perrin pushed herself onto her elbows. Everything complained—knees, shoulder, the heel of one hand scraped raw—but nothing felt broken. She flexed toes, ankles, and fingers. Pain brightened and settled. She let out a laugh that sounded too loud in the cavern. It startled her more than it should have.

"Thank you," she said, because that felt less ridiculous than screaming again.

The roots did not answer. A single drop fell somewhere behind her and ticked like a metronome.

She thought of her mother's last look—the flash of something Perrin had never seen there before, not anger, not even fear, but a kind of cracking—and swallowed hard. The watch. The engraving. The way Pandra had said He is here as if it were a fact, not a hope. The memory shivered through her the way the net had, quick and uninvited.

"Mom," Perrin whispered up into the shaft. "I'm—" The word died. Whatever the roots were, they had lifted her beyond the reach of her voice. Soundclimbed and slipped.

She rolled carefully, testing weight onto her left knee. A stab of pain turned white and then faded to a dull throb. She could move. Good. Her hands had stopped shaking. Less good: the light was already thinning as the mushrooms calmed.

She stayed still and took stock the way Grandma had taught her for kitchen mishaps and, apparently, bottomless pits: breathe first, look second. The shelf formed a narrow tongue of rock jutting over a deeper void. On thenear side, where the net had hooked, a wrinkle of roots and stone created a crawlspace big enough for her to fit. A faint draft flowed through it, cool and damp, smelling like old leaves after rain.

Down in the dark, a diffuse glow sighed from the depths—more of the blue-green, scattered and far, like a city seen through fog. She could not tell if it was down the shaft or off to one side. The vibration she'd felt earlier tickled her palms when she set them on the rock. It wasn't random. It pulsed in patterns just outside the edge of understanding, the way a language looks like noise until you learn the first word.

"Is someone there?" she called, hating the tremor in her voice.

Silence reached back. Then a soft series of clicks answered from the crawlspace, like pebbles tapping together. Perrin's scalp prickled. The clicks repeated, closer this time, and the draft lifted strands of her hair.

She wiggled toward the opening before she could talk herself out of it. The stone scraped her elbows and pressed grit into her hoodie. The tunnel narrowed, widened, curved. Her breath sounded like an animal that had followed her in. The fungus along the floor stirred and brightened at her approach, enough to paint the world in sea-glass colors. Enough to show her where not to put her hands.

Feet first, she eased down a short drop and caught herself badly with her tender palm. Stars popped behind her eyes. "Ow," she whispered into her sleeve, as if the cave might scold her for swearing.

The tunnel spat her into a chamber that sighed with light.

It wasn't bright—nothing about it felt like sunlight —but compared to the throat of the shaft, it was a revelation. Fungal shelves climbed the walls like staggered books, each lip glowing from within. Filaments fell in soft curtains and shivered at the faintest movement. Roots ribbed the ceiling and vanished into a central mound that looked, for all the world, like a knotted heart.

The vibration deepened, gentle but undeniable.

Perrin took one step onto the chamber floor.

The floor answered.

Under the thin crust of dust, roots braided and unbraided, making a subtle bowl for her weight. Not a trap. A cushion. A welcome or a test—she couldn't tell which. She wriggled her toes in her boots and felt silly for thinking a cave could have opinions.

"It's fine," she told herself, because it had to be. "It's— fine."

The chamber breathed in. The glow dimmed.

Somewhere in the far wall, something big shifted, just enough to pour a new river of shadow across the floor.

Perrin froze, the word fine shriveling in her mouth. Her scraped palm pulsed in time with the low hum. The hair along her arms lifted like a field in wind.

The shadow was not a shadow.

It unfolded from the wall with the patience of a mountain changing its mind. Plates of black—no, not black; obsidian shot through with small, cold lights—rolled over one another in rows along a flank as broad as a truck hood. A tusk the length of Perrin's arm tipped into the glow and caught it, breaking the light into knives. Air coming out of it smelled like minerals and ash, the way the world might smell before it knew fire.

She did not run. Maybe because she couldn't. Maybe because every running choice in her life lately had ended at a worse cliff.

Her breath steamed in the cooler air. The creature's eyes picked her out of the chamber and fixed there. Blue, not like a sky but like frozen depth, and reflective, so she saw a small, shaking girl cut into the center of them, ridiculous and alive.

The vibration—no longer vibration, now a tone— bloomed behind her eyes, a pressure without pain. The net had made space for her body. This sound made space for her mind, the way a hand might open to show it had nothing hidden in the palm.

If it had wanted to, it could have crushed her between

one breath and the next. Instead the tusked head lowered, just enough to be less than a threat, the way a big dog lowers itself to let a toddler touch its cheek.

Perrin swallowed. "Hi," she said, because hi was what you said when you met the neighbor's terrifying German shepherd, and because any word felt better than silence.

The tone rippled. The filaments quivered. The roots under her feet tightened their cradle by a hair.

"Okay," she breathed again, but this time it wasn't to herself.

The chamber held its breath with her.

The tusked shape kept unfolding, patient as bedrock shifting. What Perrin had first thought was wall became flank, then shoulder, then the curved plate of a massive head that scraped the chamber ceiling as it rose. Its armor was layered in obsidian hide, not smooth but scalloped, each plate etched faintly with veins of blue-white light, like frost trapped in volcanic glass. Breath gusted from its nostrils, hot and mineral-heavy, and stirred her hair back against her scalp.

The Guardian Beast. She didn't have words for it beyond that—some part of her bones named it, even if her mouth couldn't. Larger than any elephant she'd seen on documentaries, with tusks that hooked forward like scythes and eyes that burned pale as stars reflected in ice. The roots beneath her feet seemed to ripple outward in deference, bowing toward its massive frame.

Her first instinct screamed: predator. Run, hide,

C. S. DEXTER

disappear. Every nerve in her body bristled for the signal. But her legs wouldn't move, locked by a weight that wasn't fear alone. The creature was studying her—not with hunger, not even with disdain, but with the cold patience of a mountain watching a bird land on its slope.

The tone pressed harder inside her skull, not painful but insistent. Her ears rang with it, and then her thoughts bent, reshaped. A wordless voice thundered through marrow, translated not into English but into knowing:

Lost child. Of sacred blood. The Chosen.

Perrin gasped, clutching at her chest as if to cage her ribs from breaking open. The words weren't spoken aloud. They lived in her blood now, seared into her like a brand of meaning she didn't yet understand. Chosen? Blood? The weight of it left her dizzy.

The beast lowered its head further, close enough that she could see her reflection fractured across the facets of its eyes. A girl with scraped hands, dirt on her face, boots fraying at the seams—and somehow, that girl was chosen? The absurdity twisted her stomach, but the resonance didn't leave. It pulsed on, unblinking, undeniable.

She swallowed hard. "Why me?" The words scraped out hoarse, pitiful in the cavern's breadth.

The beast did not answer in language again. It simply breathed, and the roots at her feet tightened once more, holding her in place—not to trap, but tosteady. The chamber shivered with that shared silence, a silence that said th choice had already been made long before she asked the question.

Then the air changed.

A new rhythm rippled through the chamber—subtle, deliberate, almost like hands clapping in slow counterpoint to the Beast's resonance. The glow in the fungal shelves wavered, dimmed, then steadied again. Roots along the walls lifted slightly, listening. From a cleft in the rock behind the beast, a figure stepped forward.

He was tall, broad-shouldered, the kind of presence that made the cavern shrink around him instead of the other way. His skin caught the blue-green glow and turned it bronze; his dark hair was tied back at the nape with a strip of woven fiber. His hands moved in slow arcs, tracing symbols Perrin didn't recognize, but the Beast responded—the tusked head lowered further, breath easing, the tension in its plated shoulders loosening.

Perrin blinked hard, throat tight. Who was he? Not another hallucination. Not Eric—this was someone anchored in this place, someone who belonged.

The figure's voice carried low but firm, layered with a timbre that seemed to harmonize with the cavern's hum. "Guardian. The child is not foe."

The Beast rumbled in reply, the vibration softening until it became less command and more acknowledgment. Its eyes broke from Perrin to the man, then back to her again. The resonance in her chest dulled from thunder to steady drumbeat.

Perrin sucked in air she hadn't realized she'd been rationing. Her knees wobbled and nearly gave, but she locked them stubbornly. She would not collapse like some fainting Victorian in front of this stranger, even if her heart wanted to.

The man approached, still moving his hands in slow gestures until the Beast finally stepped back, plates grinding like glaciers shifting. Its bulk melted into the shadows, leaving only the echo of its breath and the cavern's dim blue glow.

Now there was only the boy—no, not a boy, older than her, but not a man yet either. Perrin's eyes caught the faint scar across his forearm, the steady lines of someone trained, disciplined. His gaze found hers, direct and unwavering. And there, for the first time since the fall, something warm—not the heat of the Beast's breath, but human.

"You should not be standing," he said quietly, in accented English that made every word careful. "But Miketo holds you."

Her lips parted. A hundred questions fought in her throat, but none came out. She only knew her face burned, not from the cold.

"Who—who are you?" she managed at last.

He hesitated, as though the answer mattered. Then: "Garantuke."

The name fit him, rooted like the cavern itself. He

extended a hand, not to shake but to steady. She stared at it, scraped palm throbbing, pride tangling with the pull of gravity. For the first time since she'd fallen, Perrin realized she wasn't alone—and that realization was as terrifying as the Beast itself.

The roots beneath Perrin shifted again, withdrawing slowly into the cavern walls until her weight was fully on her own legs. The moment they released her, pain surged sharp and hot through her knee. She staggered, sucking air between her teeth. Her scraped hand burned, and a dull ache rolled up her shoulder where she'd hit the stone. The adrenaline that had kept her upright bled away all at once, leaving her trembling.

"Stay still," Garantuke said, his voice even but not unkind. He stepped closer, hand hovering near her elbow without yet touching, like he knew she would flinch if he moved too fast.

"I'm fine," Perrin blurted, though her voice cracked around the word. She tried to straighten her spine, tried to act like the fall and the Beast and the pain hadn't hollowed her out. But when she took a step, her left leg folded, and she had to catch herself against the wall.

Garantuke's brow tightened. He made a motion with his hand—another of those slow, deliberate gestures— and the cavern seemed to hush in response. The light along the fungal shelves steadied, brighter for a moment, as if listening to him.

"You are hurt," he said simply.

Perrin shook her head hard, embarrassment pricking hotter than her scraped skin. "I can walk. I don't need—"

But her voice wavered again, and when she pushed off the wall, her ankle betrayed her with another sharp bolt of pain. She hissed, clamping her jaw shut against the sound.

Garantuke's hand was at her elbow now, steady, firm. Not asking permission anymore. "You will make it worse."

Her pride screamed no, but her body leaned into his grip before she could stop it. He bent, sliding an arm behind her knees and another around her back, lifting her in one clean motion. She gasped, arms reflexively clutching his shoulders. The warmth of him cut against the cavern chill, startling and too close.

"Put me down," she muttered, though her voice was small. Her face was hot enough to glow brighter than the fungi.

Garantuke's expression didn't change. He adjusted her weight easily, as if she were a bundle of reeds, and started walking. The roots along the ground unwove ahead of him, forming a clear path, then braided back once he passed.

Perrin squirmed once, testing his hold, but the pain in her knee screamed louder than her stubbornness. She slumped against him with a frustrated sigh. "Fine. But only until I can walk."

He gave no answer, though she felt the faintest shift of

breath that might have been amusement. His stride was steady, unhurried, carrying her deeper into the glow of the cavern—and despite herself, Perrin let her head tip briefly against his shoulder, the fight bleeding out of her as the underground world opened ahead.

The passage widened by degrees until the ceiling arched high above them, ribbed with roots that shimmered faintly as if lit from within. Perrin blinked hard, thinking at first that her eyes had tricked her. But no —the glow was real, and it multiplied.

What opened before her was no simple cave. It was a city hidden in the earth.

Crops grew in terraces along the cavern walls—stalks with translucent husks that shimmered like stained glass, fungi the size of umbrellas fanning open in pools of still water, and vines heavy with fruits that glowed softly from within. Bridges of living roots stretched between ledges, bowing and tightening as villagers crossed, each step met with a pulse of light. Children darted across the bridges, their laughter rising like birdsong under the stone vault. Animals Perrin couldn't name—shapes like deer but antlered with coral, birds feathered in gems— moved through the glowing groves.

Everywhere, life hummed with that same deep vibration she had felt since her fall, like the whole village shared a heartbeat with the roots that held it together.

Perrin forgot for a moment about her throbbing knee, about the boy carrying her as if she weighed nothing.

She pushed herself up slightly in Garantuke's arms, wide-eyed. "This is... this is real?"

His gaze stayed forward, but his voice was calm,

Garantuke carried her through the cavern's glowing arteries until the paths converged at a wide chamber. Perrin blinked against the brightness—walls clad in moss that shimmered as though lit from within, pools lined with root-tangles that pulsed like veins. It smelled of earth after rain, sharp with minerals, threaded with something sweeter, almost floral. Voices hushed as they entered.

Villagers stood in a half-circle, tall and broad-shouldered, their clothes woven from fiber that glowed faintly in patterns of vines and waves. Some whispered; some frowned. Perrin caught fragments she couldn't quite translate, but the tone was clear enough—distrust, suspicion, and something like awe.

Garantuke set her down on a bed of soft moss. The moment her weight left his arms, her knee screamed again, and she sucked in air through her teeth. Before she could push a joke past the pain, an elder knelt beside her, hair streaked silver, palms scarred with old burns. Without a word, he pressed both hands just above her wound.

The cavern answered.

Light threaded through the moss, rising in filaments, and crawled over her skin like static come alive. It spread, tendrils of blue-white energy weaving into her leg, her shoulder, her scraped palm. Warmth at first—comforting, like a bath after cold rain—then sharper, invasive, burrowing into places no hand should reach. Perrin gasped, jerking, but Garantuke steadied her with a hand at her shoulder.

"Breathe," he said quietly.

She tried. The warmth turned to heat, then to pressure that felt like her bones were being tested for cracks and flaws. Her thoughts blurred; her body wasn't hers. She saw flashes—roots splitting stone, water rushing underground, the glow of fungi blooming in slow motion. A rhythm pressed into her chest, the same vibration she had felt since falling, but now it lived inside her heartbeat.

The elder's voice intoned something low, syllables that tangled like vines. The villagers echoed in whispers, their tones layering until the chamber itself seemed to chant. Perrin clutched the moss, nails digging in, torn between awe and panic.

Then—release.

The light snapped back into the moss with a shiver. The elder leaned away, sweat beading his brow. Perrin's breath tore free. The pain in her knee was gone. Her shoulder felt... whole. The scraped palm shone pink and new, like a healed scar only moments old.

She stared at her hands, flexed her knee, and pressed weight into it. Perfect. Too perfect. Her chest heaved.

"That wasn't—" She swallowed. "That wasn't healing.

That was—"

"Invasive," Garantuke finished for her, his expression unreadable. "Miketo leaves nothing hidden. It knows what we are."

Perrin pulled her arms close, shivering despite the warmth left in her veins. "I didn't ask for that."

"No one does," said another villager from the circle. Murmurs rippled—half reverent, half wary. "It gives where it wills. It takes where it must."

The whispers swelled again, eyes flicking to Perrin. Stranger. Outsider. And yet—marked. A girl the Guardian Beast had spared. A girl Miketo had touched without permission.

Garantuke glanced at her, jaw tight, then addressed the circle: "She survived what should kill. The Guardian lowered its head. Miketo has spoken."

That silenced the chamber for a moment—but only a moment. The murmurs returned, thicker now, distrust sharpening into open fear.

Perrin's stomach knotted. She didn't understand their words, but she knew what it felt like to be pointed at. To be the story whispered at someone else's table. And she hated that even here, in a glowing world under the earth, she was still the joke nobody trusted.

The chamber's murmurs thickened until they were almost a single voice, layered and sharp. Perrin caught the words even if she couldn't translate them: outsider, danger, cursed. One woman spat on the floor. A man crossed his arms and muttered low, shaking his head. Others whispered in awe, fingers pointing toward her healed skin, the faint glow that still clung to her hair as if Miketo hadn't quite finished with her.

Her stomach sank. She curled her hands into fists, nails pressing crescents into her palms, wishing she could shrink small enough to vanish into the moss.

Garantuke stepped forward, his shoulders squared, his stance like a wall between her and the half-circle of distrust. His eyes swept the villagers, steady, unflinching. The crowd quieted—not silenced, but pressed back by the weight of his presence.

"She should not have survived," he said, voice carrying low and certain. The words weren't praise. They landed like a judgment, like a law being recited. "The fall kills. The Guardian kills. Miketo punishes those who offend it. Yet she stands."

The villagers shifted, restless. Some looked away. Others glared harder, as though his truth threatened what they believed. Perrin's throat tightened. Was that supposed to comfort her? That she had broken some rule of nature by living through this?

Garantuke turned, his gaze meeting hers. His expression was unreadable—hard, but not cruel. "You are marked now," he said, softer, pitched for her alone. "That can be a gift. Or it can be a death sentence. Which one—it is not my choice. It is yours."

The words rooted in her chest heavier than the healing

had. She couldn't find an answer, not with so many eyes on her, not with his watching too. She only nodded once, small and stiff, though her mind screamed she wasn't ready for any of this.

Around her, the whispers continued, ebbing and flowing like a tide stop. Above them all, the moss-light pulsed once, dimmed, and held steady—as if Miketo itself were waiting to see what she would do next.

CHAPTER 5: MOONSHADOW'S WARNING

Perrin woke with a start, her breath catching in her throat. For a disorienting moment she thought she was still falling, body twisting through darkness—but no. She was lying on a bed of moss, cool and springy beneath her, a faint glow seeping up through the fibers like starlight caught in green. Her hands flew to her knee, her shoulder, the palm she'd scraped raw during the fall.

Smooth. Whole. Not even a bruise.

Her heart hammered. She sat up too fast, dizzy with the realization that she wasn't broken. Not even sore. Every ache from the mine, every sting from the collapse, gone like they'd never existed. She touched her face, her arms, testing herself, searching for the pain she remembered. Nothing.

But the memory of the healing ritual clung to her like damp cloth—the rush of energy crawling through her veins, the sense that something alien had unstitched and rewoven her from the inside out. It had felt like drowning and breathing at once, like being seen too closely by something that had no eyes.

She pressed her palms against her stomach, shivering. "That wasn't just healing," she whispered to herself. "That was... something else."

Outside her chamber, muffled voices passed—a laugh, the scrape of a basket being set down, the faint flutter of wings. The sounds of a village alive. Perrin stayed where she was, unsure if she wanted to see what waited beyond the moss walls. Healed or not, her body felt like it belonged to someone else now.

And she couldn't shake the question burning in her chest: why had Miketo saved her at all?

Perrin pushed herself up from the moss bed, her legs trembling more from nerves than weakness. The walls of her chamber opened into a sloping arch of woven roots, glowing faintly as if lit from within. She brushed her fingers along them as she stepped out, half afraid they would recoil. Instead, the roots shifted gently, parting to form a doorway into the village beyond.

The sight stole her breath.

Tuspin stretched before her like something dreamt into being: terraces of glowing crops nestled in layers of stone, their leaves shimmering with veins of light. Bridges of thick, braided roots arched across pools of bioluminescent water, swaying faintly as villagers crossed them. Massive butterflies—wings the size of dinner plates—drifted overhead, trailing dust that gleamed like sparks. And above it all, faint motes drifted through the cavern air, painting everything in a haze of gold and green.

She stood frozen at the threshold, her mouth slightly open. This wasn't a village—it was a living heartbeat beneath the earth.

A sharp chirrup startled her. She turned just in time to see a bird—its feathers like shards of emerald and sapphire—perch on a nearby post. It tilted its head, then mimicked her gasp exactly, the sound eerie in its precision. Perrin flushed. "Really?" she muttered. The bird chirruped again, copying her tone perfectly, then fluttered off with a spray of glowing feathers.

Everywhere she looked, life responded to the people moving among it. Roots shifted under villagers' feet to form new paths. A basket hung from a branch, lowered by vines into waiting hands. Children laughed as a patch of glowing fungi pulsed brighter beneath their play, as though the cavern itself were joining their game.

Perrin hugged her arms around herself. The place was beautiful, yes—but it was alive in ways that made her skin prickle. Nothing in this world stayed still, not even the ground under her boots. And the thought needled at her: if everything here responded to intent, what did it see in her?

Perrin lingered at the edge of the root-bridge, staring at the glowing crops as if they might vanish if she blinked. Her awe held until she noticed a shadow moving toward her, broad-shouldered and steady. Garantuke.

His expression was not softened by the glow of Tuspin. His eyes fixed on her, sharp as flint, and when he stopped a few feet away the air between them felt suddenly heavy.

"You should not be walking," he said. His voice carried the low, steady weight of someone accustomed to being obeyed. "The healers finished only hours ago."

"I feel fine," Perrin said quickly, too quickly. She straightened her shoulders, though the memory of the ritual still itched under her skin. "Better than fine, actually."

"That is not the point." Garantuke stepped closer, gaze flicking to the moss-light still clinging faintly to her skin. "Do you understand what happened? Falls like yours break spines. The Guardian would have ended you if not for Miketo's will. And yet you stand here, as if the laws of this world can be ignored."

Perrin's throat tightened. "I didn't ask to survive," she snapped, then regretted the sharpness in her voice. "I mean—I didn't know what would happen."

He looked at her for a long moment, unreadable. Then he exhaled through his nose, a sound of frustration more than anger. "Recklessness is not bravery. Miketo sees the difference. And if it decides your foolishness endangers Tuspin, it will not punish you alone."

The words struck harder than she expected. Perrin's

stomach hollowed. She wanted to argue, to defend herself, but her voice faltered. "So what—you think I'm a curse?"

Garantuke's jaw tightened. "I think you are an unknown. Unknowns are dangerous. You survived when you should not have, and that means a reckoning will come. For you... and perhaps for all of us."

He turned, his movements precise, disciplined, and walked back toward the central terraces. Perrin stood frozen, heat rising in her face though the cavern air was cool. The butterflies still drifted lazily overhead, the roots still shifted, the villagers still moved as if nothing had changed.

But for Perrin, the beauty of Tuspin now carried teeth.

The sting of Garantuke's words clung to Perrin as she wandered farther into the cavern. She tried to lose herself in the bustle of Tuspin—the hum of voices, the faint music of water trickling down stone, the rhythmic creak of woven root bridges swaying underfoot. But nothing muted the echo in her mind: *Recklessness is not bravery.*

She stopped near a shallow pool where light rippled across the surface like liquid stars. Her reflection bent and shimmered, making her look like someone else entirely— stronger, stranger, maybe even dangerous. She crouched, brushing her fingers across the cool water.

"You don't belong here."

The voice came from behind her, soft as smoke. Perrin whirled.

A woman stood there where no one had been a breath before. Skin pale bluelike moonlight on ice, eyes luminous and endless, hair drifting as if stirred by an unseen current. She wasn't dressed like the villagers—no woven moss or root leathers. Her robe clung and flowed all at once, threaded with symbols Perrin couldn't read but somehow felt in her chest.

Perrin's breath caught. "Who—?"

"Moonshadow," the woman said, her voice carrying a weight that made the cavern itself seem to listen. She stepped closer, gaze piercing. "Eric is Malum."

The words hit Perrin harder than a shove. "What?"

"He is not what he pretends to be," Moonshadow continued, each syllable deliberate. "He is Malum. The voice that consumes. The shadow that commands."

Perrin's mouth went dry. Her heart lurched against her ribs, memories flooding—Eric's hand gesture on the school steps, the compulsion in his voice, the fog that had rolled into her skull without warning. "I knew he was... wrong. But Malum? What does that even mean?"

Moonshadow tilted her head, eyes narrowing in sympathy and warning all at once. "It means he will not stop until you are broken. Unless you learn. Unless you listen. Do not travel the Allekanu Path, for you shall encounter the Contrary Men that have been altered by Malum."

Before Perrin could demand answers, the woman's outline began to thin, dissolving into the cavern air like mist caught in wind. "Wait—don't go!" Perrin reached out, but her hand met only empty air.

A pair of villagers passed on the far side of the pool, carrying baskets of luminous fungi. Perrin rushed to them. "Did you see her? The woman who was just here?"

They exchanged blank looks. "Who, child?"

"The one with blue skin! Right here, she was standing right here—"

Their faces stayed empty, unconcerned. One of them gave her a sympathetic frown before walking on. The other shook their head. "You should rest. The healing has left you dazed."

Perrin stared at the empty space where Moonshadow had been, her chest tightening. She wasn't crazy. She couldn't be. But if no one else had seen her...then why had Moonshadow chosen only her?

Perrin backed away from the pool, pulse racing, Moonshadow's words clanging in her skull like struck bells. Eric is Malum. It felt too big, too heavy to hold alone, but the villagers' blank stares told her she was holding it alone whether she wanted to or not.

She didn't realize she had wandered into the training grounds until a line of glowing runes underfoot caught her eye. The circle of stone was broad and worn smooth, framed by root-torches that pulsed with a living green fire. Inside the circle, Garantuke stood with two others: Selena, her features calm but watchful, and Kimilo, whose posture was sharp enough to cut.

"You're late," Kimilo said, her voice crisp, like she'd been waiting for her. "We were about to begin without you."

Perrin blinked. "Begin what?"

"Your instruction," Selena answered, her tone gentler. "If you are to remain here, you must understand Miketo. Ignorance is more dangerous than weakness."

Garantuke's eyes found hers, hard as before but steadier now. "Listen well. This is no game. The power that spared you can destroy you if you treat it lightly."

Perrin shifted uneasily. "I didn't... treat it lightly. I just —"

"Fell," Kimilo interrupted. "Yes. And yet you lived. That is no small thing. It means Miketo marked you. But a mark is not a gift freely given. It is a test."

Selena lifted her hand, and in her palm swirled a faint purple whirlwind, its light curling around her fingers like affectionate smoke. Perrin gasped, the tiny storm alive in a way no trick could imitate. Selena smiled, though there was a flicker of hesitation in her eyes, as if baring this power cost her something. "Miketo is not a tool," she said. "It is conscious. It is energy that listens—electric, heat, kinetic, spirit, thought. It gives when respected. It punishes when abused."

Kimilo's voice cut in, sharp where Selena's was soft. "Rule one: you cannot force it. Rule two: it mirrors you. Rage births destruction. Fear feeds weakness. Rule three: arrogance calls punishment. If you forget, you won't have to wait for enemies to end you—Miketo will do it first."

Perrin swallowed hard, remembering Garantuke's warning. "And what if I don't... want it?"

Garantuke stepped closer, his shadow falling across her. "Then it will not matter what you want. Miketo chose to spare you. It will watch you now, weighing every step. Whether you rise or fall, it will not look away."

The cavern seemed to pulse around her at his words, the runes beneath her feet glowing faintly as if in agreement. Perrin's hands curled into fists. Chosen or not, she hated the feeling of being measured by something she couldn't see.

Perrin's stomach twisted under their words, but part of her bristled too. She had always been told what she couldn't do—by teachers, by her mom, by kids who thought she was nothing but a punchline. Now here were three more people, telling her to be careful, to go slow, to think. The weight of it pressed down until the only thing she wanted was to push back.

"So what, you just... ask nicely?" she said, folding her arms. "Seems like power with too many strings attached."

Kimilo's sharp gaze cut across the circle. Her hair, black and neatly bound, caught the glow of the root-torches. "It is not power. It is a listener. Speak without respect, and you are answered without mercy."

Perrin's jaw tightened. "Maybe I should try for myself."

"Don't," Garantuke warned immediately, his tone edged. "Not until you are guided."

But the more he said no, the more something reckless inside her screamed yes. Perrin stepped into the center of the ring, fists curling. She thought of the glow in Selena's hand, the storm that had twined so elegantly around her fingers. Perrin wanted that. Needed that.

She closed her eyes, reaching out with nothing but raw want. Heat prickled along her arms. The runes underfoot brightened. For an instant, she thought she had it— energy gathering in her chest, racing to her fingertips like a spark ready to ignite.

She thrust her hand forward.

The spark shattered. The glow snapped back, slamming into her chest like a hammer. Perrin cried out, flung backward into the dust at the ring's edge. The impact rattled her teeth and left her ribs aching. Smoke curled faintly from her palm.

Selena knelt beside her in an instant, hands hovering but not touching. "Are you hurt?"

Perrin coughed, forcing herself upright, though her pride stung more than her body. "I—I almost had it."

Kimilo's voice was cool, precise. "No. You had nothing. You reached with arrogance. Miketo showed you the price."

Garantuke's eyes locked on hers, hard and unreadable. "If that had been the Belofez watching, you'd already be dead."

The word hung in the air like a blade. Perrin hugged her stinging hand to her chest, biting down the urge to argue. For once, she had no clever retort—only the burning truth that she had failed again, and this time the cost might have been far worse than humiliation.

"What is the Belofez?" Perrin asked calmly.

Kimilo stared with shock at Perrin. "It is a huge creature. Fast and deadly. It's body impenetrable. Faster than you can blink, it's tongue can dart out grab several men and eat them whole."

The training circle emptied into uneasy silence after Perrin's collapse. Selena helped her to her feet, but even her gentle hand on Perrin's shoulder couldn't soften the atmosphere. Villagers had gathered along the edge of the ring—men and women who had come at the sound of her cry, eyes narrowed, whispers already starting. Selena led to a nearby building with Kimilo and Garantuke following.

The Hall of Scrolls was nothing like the training circle. Its walls soared high, lined with shelves grown from the roots themselves, each cradling bundles of reed parchment, stone tablets, and woven records that glowed faintly with Miketo's touch. The air smelled of dust and something older than dust, like a library that remembered every word ever spoken within it.

Perrin stood in the center of the chamber, flanked by Selena and Kimilo, while Garantuke lingered a few paces back, his arms folded tight. Above, root-lamps shed pale light across a half-circle of elders seated on carved stone benches. Their robes shimmered with threadlike veins of light, marking each of them as voices of authority.

"She should not remain," said the silver-braided elder, voice sharp as flint. "Already her arrogance stirs the ground. What happens when she fails again? Will Tuspin pay the price?"

"She is a child," countered the elder woman with the lined face, her tone steady. "And yet she lived when she should have died. That is not accident—it is intent."

The chamber filled with rising voices, some brittle with fear, others heavy with suspicion.

"Surface-born, rash, foolish—"

"She attracts calamity—"

"Or perhaps she survived because she was meant to—"

"Meant to doom us!"

Each word landed on Perrin like stones, pressing her smaller and smaller. Her throat tightened. She wanted to argue, to say she hadn't asked for any of this, but the heat of so many eyes froze the words in her chest.

"Expel her before she dooms us all!" someone cried.

"Train her before her recklessness dooms her!" another snapped back.

The debate tangled into a storm, voices overlapping, hands slicing the air. Perrin swayed where she stood, fighting the urge to bolt for the doors. She had never felt so much like the punchline of her own life—out of place, unwanted, about to be cast away.

Selena's hand brushed hers, grounding her. Kimilo's gaze flicked toward her too, sharp but not unkind. Even

Garantuke's silence at her back was a weight she clung to. Still, the tide of voices made her stomach sink. She was one vote away from being tossed back into the dark.

And then—silence.

A figure stood among the roots at the edge of the chamber, pale blue skin glowing faintly in the dim. Moonshadow. She hadn't entered—she had simply been there, as though the scrolls themselves had given her shape.

Every voice stilled. Some elders lowered their heads. Others simply stared.

Moonshadow's eyes fixed on Perrin. Her voice was low, but it filled the Hall like it had been waiting for centuries to be heard. "Graywun's blood."

The words slammed through the chamber. Gasps rippled the benches. The silver-braided elder's mouth snapped shut mid-argument. Even the roots seemed to pulse once, their glow flickering like a held breath.

Perrin's pulse hammered in her ears. Graywun. Her grandmother's name—but not like she'd ever heard it before, not like a secret nickname whispered at bedtime. This was a title, heavy as armor, fierce as flame.

Moonshadow stepped closer, her presence bending the air. "She is no accident. She is the granddaughter of Graywun—the liberator, breaker of chains, hunter of devils. Will you cast aside what Miketo has already spared?"

Shock rooted the elders in place. The arguments died

in their throats. Selena's breath caught audibly beside her. Kimilo's dark eyes narrowed, not in scorn but in calculation. Behind her, Perrin felt Garantuke stiffen like a bowstring.

Perrin's knees wobbled. She barely understood the words, but she understood their weight. Her grandmother—Grandma Grace—was more than she had ever admitted. And now, somehow, that legacy pressed down on Perrin's shoulders like a cloak too heavy to wear.

Moonshadow's gaze lingered on her one last time. "Train her. Or answer for it when the shadow rises."

Her form blurred, edges dissolving like smoke. In the space of a blink, she was gone.

The chamber remained stunned, the silence louder than the shouting had been. Perrin stood trembling, the name Graywun echoing through her bones, a destiny she didn't ask for settling over her like stone. She lowered her gaze, but even with her eyes on the floor she could feel every elder's stare, weighing her, measuring her, already expecting more than she knew how to give. Garantuke took a scroll and open it for Perrin to see. On it were enormous lizards with extremely long tongues grabbing warriors and destroying buildings. It was frightening.

Garantuke rolled the scroll together again. "Those are the Belofez. That is what we seek to avoid."

For the first time since she'd fallen into this strange world, Perrin wished she could disappear back into the darkness. But something deep inside whispered that there was no going back—not after this.

CHAPTER 6: THE FORBIDDEN PATH

Perrin lay on her side in the woven cot, staring at the faint bioluminescent glow that pulsed from the fungus-veins in the wall. Each pulse seemed louder than the last, like the whole cavern was counting down just to taunt her. Sleep wasn't happening. Not when every whispered argument from the Hall of Scrolls still spun in her ears.

Reckless. Unwanted. Graywun's blood.

She rolled over and pressed her cheek into the blanket, but that only made her stomach knot tighter. Everyone in this world thought they had her figured out—fragile, dangerous, destined. Nobody had asked what she wanted. Nobody had seen what she could do.

Her hand brushed the wooden Miketo traing staff leaning against the wall. It thrummed faintly under her fingertips, not quite alive, not quite still. The sensation made her skin prickle. It was supposed to help her, wasn't it? Supposed to mean she wasn't useless. Yet all she'd managed so far was to fumble, to fail, to make Garantuke's jaw clench every time she spoke.

"I'm not waiting around to be babysat," she whispered.

The village outside was hushed, the fungal gardens casting their eerie glow across the cavern floor. She listened—no footsteps, no voices, just the faint hum of water moving through roots somewhere below. Carefully, she slipped her boots on, tied the laces tight, and lifted the staff.

One breath. Then another.

Perrin ducked under the hanging root that marked her chamber door, heart hammering as though the whole cavern could hear it. Each step down the winding walkway made her pulse race faster, but no alarm was raised. The bridges were empty, the air cool and damp. Everyone else trusted the safety of Tuspin.

She didn't. Not anymore.

At the far end of the cavern, the roots parted into the Allekanu Path. She'd heard the name whispered like a warning by Moonshadow, the place she told her *not* to travel. Which, of course, made it the only place she could imagine going.

She squared her shoulders, muttered, "They'll see I can handle this," and slipped into the shadows of the Path.

The Allekanu Path breathed like a throat cut into the earth. The further Perrin went, the more the air pressed against her skin, damp and heavy, like it wanted her to turn around.

The walls leaned close, slick with mineral sweat, etched with spirals that seemed to move when she wasn't looking. They weren't painted—they glowed, faint lines of green-white light sinking into the rock itself. Perrin reached out once, brushing her fingers over the nearest curve. The stone felt cold, but her fingertips tingled as if the spiral had exhaled into her nerves.

She yanked her hand back, her pulse leaping.

The deeper she went, the louder the whispers grew. At first they were faint, like kids whispering behind cupped hands in class. Then they sharpened—halfwords, fractured phrases, all echoing just out of reach of understanding.

"Too small..." "Turn back..." "...Graywun's blood spilled..."

She clamped her hands over her ears. The whispers didn't stop. They were inside the rock, inside her head.

Her throat tightened. This wasn't the time to freak out. She'd snuck here to prove herself, not to collapse in some creepy hallway like a scared little kid.

"Shut up," she hissed. The sound of her own voice steadied her, even if her knees shook. "I'm not turning back."

Her staff thrummed faintly, as if agreeing—or warning. She gritted her teeth and kept walking, eyes on the spirals winding deeper and deeper into the dark.

And then the air shifted. The glow from the spirals bent strangely, like light bending through water, and ahead came the sound of... footsteps. Not ordinary ones. A syncopated shuffle, backward and wrong.

Something waited in the Path.

The shuffle became clearer the further Perrin crept—like shoes scuffing the stone, but not in any rhythm she recognized. One step scraped, then another jumped, then a third landed as if the walker's legs didn't know forward from back.

Then they appeared.

At first, Perrin thought she'd stumbled onto a costume party no one had invited her to. Three tall men stood in the glow of the spirals, dressed like they'd crawled out of a sepia photograph: beige vests buttoned snug, long coat-tails brushing the back of their knees, black boots polished to a shine that caught the glow. And on each head, perched absurdly straight, were top hats.

Perrin blinked. "Seriously?"

One of the men turned—except his body twisted the wrong way, pivoting backward until his face, pale and slack, angled toward her. His lips moved, fast, garbled:

"!uoy truh yllaer ot desoppus er'eW"

The words tumbled out so quickly they rattled like marbles. She didn't catch them until her brain, straining, rewound them in her head.

We're supposed to really hurt you!

Perrin's stomach lurched. Backwards. They were talking backwards.

Another man bounced in a little hop—backward, of course—then lifted his gloved hand. Energy pooled in his palm, swirling into a ball of pale light that looked harmless until it snapped like a live wire. With a flick, he hurled it past Perrin's shoulder. It struck the wall behind her with a crack, splattering pain into the stone like an invisible bruise. The glow spirals dimmed around the impact as if recoiling.

The third man laughed—or maybe cried. The sound came out warped, high and low at once, crawling down Perrin's spine. He spoke too, a rapid backward spill:

"!rewop ruoy esu ot yrT"

Her chest tightened as the meaning clicked. *Try to use your power!*

They were mocking her. Daring her.

Perrin gripped her staff tighter, trying to steady her breath. Her throat was dry, but her pride burned hotter. "Fine," she muttered. "You want me to try? Watch me."

The Contrary Men grinned—all three, in eerie unison —then began to circle her, hopping and stepping backward like dancers rehearsing the same unsettling choreography. The spirals on the walls pulsed faster, feeding the pressure that built in her chest.

The Contrary Men's backward circling pressed her deeper into the Path, her boots crunching grit she hadn't noticed before. Then the narrow stone throat widened, spilling out into a cavern so vast it made her dizzy.

Across the abyss, rising from the stone like a black tooth, was a fortress.

Its walls gleamed with a slick sheen, as if someone had poured molten obsidian into shape and let it harden into towers and arches. Unnatural firelight flickered from windows too tall and narrow, throwing shadows that stretched and bent across the cavern floor. A single bridge of dark stone connected the fortress gate to the far ledge, suspended over nothing.

Even at this distance Perrin felt it staring at her, the whole thing alive somehow, waiting.

Her breath caught. "Eric..." she whispered.

As if the name were a cue, the Contrary Men stopped their circling. In eerie synchronicity, they turned their heads—backward, always backward—toward the fortress. Then, one by one, they looked at her again, grins sharpening.

The nearest man spat another tangle of reversed words, fast and mocking: "!niaga meht toohs ot emit s'ti wonk uoY"

Her brain flipped it with a shiver: *You know it's time to shoot them again!*

The others answered with a chorus of warped laughter, bouncing in jagged hops. The energy spheres reappeared in their hands, crackling like miniature suns ready to bruise flesh.

Perrin's chest thudded. The fortress loomed, daring her. The men dared her. Her pride roared back louder than her fear.

She lifted the Miketo staff, its faint hum rising into her bones. "You think I'm scared of you?" she snapped, her voice trembling only at the edges. "Let's see how you like this."

The staff thrummed like a laser wanting to go rogue in Perrin's grip, warmth rising up the wood as if it were filling itself with breath. She planted her feet the way she remembered Garantuke doing, angled the staff toward the nearest Contrary Man, and shoved every scrap of focus she had into the word she thought *might* command it.

"Strike!"

A flash ripped from the staff's tip, white-blue and blinding. For a heartbeat, triumph soared through her— she'd done it, she was actually using Miketo.

Then the blast slammed into the man's chest, and everything went wrong.

Instead of burning him, the light warped and folded like elastic, then snapped back. The orb of energy ricocheted off his coat with a sound like breaking glass, screaming straight into Perrin's ribs.

The impact lifted her off her feet.

Pain bloomed sharp and hot, flaring across her side like someone had pressed a branding iron there. She hit the ground hard, her staff clattering away, her breath knocked out in a humiliating wheeze.

The Contrary Men clapped in unison, the sound sharp and backward, their laughter a garbled echo of playground mockery. One mimicked her fall, staggering backward, clutching his side in exaggerated agony, then hopping up with a jeer.

Perrin curled on her side, gasping, her eyes watering. The staff lay just out of reach, humming faintly as if disappointed. She stretched toward it, but her fingers shook too much to close the gap.

You're nothing, the whispers in the walls hissed. *Not chosen. Foolish child.*

Her pride cracked under the pain. Her chest heaved once, twice, and then she did the only thing left: she scrambled up on her hands and knees and ran.

Her side screamed with every step, but Perrin forced her legs to move. The Path tilted and blurred under her feet as she staggered, half-running, half-limping back the way she had come.

Behind her, the Contrary Men laughed. Not loud, not chasing—just that eerie backward chorus, bouncing and clapping as if she'd been the entertainment. Their mockery clung to the cavern walls, echoing in warped syllables until it felt like the air itself was jeering.

She risked a glance over her shoulder. They hadn't followed. They didn't need to. Their crooked silhouettes stood framed against the fortress light, top hats bobbing as they jerked in their unsettling half-dance, like puppets without strings. One of them raised a gloved hand and gave a slow, backward wave that somehow looked like a dismissal.

Heat burned Perrin's cheeks. She wanted to scream at them, to spit something clever back, but her lungs only coughed ragged breaths. The shame pressed harder than the pain in her ribs.

When she finally stumbled back into the glow of Tuspin's outer roots, her knees buckled. She braced against the living wood, gulping air, trying to swallow the sob that threatened to tear loose. She'd gone out to prove herself, to show she wasn't some reckless child—and all she had to show for it was bruises, humiliation, and the laughter of monsters still ringing in her ears.

Perrin pressed herself against the root wall, chest heaving. Her hands were empty. The shame of it bit hard —she hadn't just failed, she'd left the staff behind like a coward.

Then came the sound.

Footsteps, but wrong—heels striking in reverse, echoing out of step with the rhythm of the cavern. She froze, every muscle stiff.

A shape slid into the edge of the glow. A Contrary Man.

Top hat, beige vest, coat tails brushing the ground. His posture tilted backward, as if the air itself pulled him the wrong way. Every warning from Garantuke screamed in Perrin's ears: *Don't let them close.*

She braced to run again, but stopped.

His hand lifted. Not to conjure one of those brutal energy spheres. Not to claw at her.

He was holding her staff.

The glowing wood rested across his palm like an offering. He stepped—backward, always backward—until he was close enough to extend it toward her. His gloved fingers trembled, as though the effort cost him.

Perrin's breath hitched. This was a trick. It had to be. But her hand moved before her brain caught up, snatching the staff back. It was warm, humming faintly, as if it had never left her.

The Contrary Man's mouth pulled into a smile too wide, too rigid. But his eyes—his eyes weren't empty. They locked on hers, and something flickered there. Something sharp and aching.

".uoy teem ot eciN" The sound cracked out of him, strangled, as though the name fought through a wall of glass.

Nice to meet you. Perrin froze. No one else had said anything like that down here.

The man's body jerked once, like an invisible leash snapped him backward. But still he lingered, gaze pleading, voice spilling fast, garbled syllables: "!meht hctaw lliw I tub uoy ees lliw I"

The words tumbled too quick, backwards, broken. She only caught fragments. *See you... watch them.*

Nonsense—but the way his voice broke on *see you* made her chest twist.

Then, with a shudder that rattled his whole frame, he turned. Backward steps carried him into the dark. His hat bobbed once, then was gone.

Perrin clutched the staff to her chest. It should have felt like comfort, but instead it pressed like a weight. Because she knew—whoever that man was, he hadn't meant her harm. Not tonight.

And that, somehow, was the most terrifying part of all.

"Perrin!"

His voice cracked across the stone like a whip.

She jerked around, clutching the staff so tight her knuckles hurt. Garantuke stormed out of the shadows, his broad shoulders filling the narrow passage, the glow from the fungi sharpening the hard lines of his face.

"What were you thinking?" His voice thundered, echoing so loud it hurt.

"I—" She tried, but the words died.

"You left Tuspin in the dead of night," he cut over her, "without training, without permission. You could have died out here." His eyes flicked to her burns, the blood smudged on her knee, the tremor in her grip on the staff. "You nearly did."

The heat behind her eyes burned, but she forced her chin up. "I just wanted to—"

"To what? Prove yourself?" He stepped closer, and she felt small, pinned under the weight of his anger. "Miketo is not a game for your pride. It is a living power. You treat it like a toy, it will kill you—and worse, it will punish all of us with you."

His words struck harder than the Contrary Men's spheres. Perrin bit down on the sob pushing up her throat.

"I'm sorry," she whispered. It sounded pitiful even to her.

Garantuke's jaw clenched, his hands curling into fists before he forced them open again. His voice dropped, lower but no softer. "If you'd died on the Path, Tuspin would have bled for your mistake. Do you understand that?"

She wanted to argue, to shout that she hadn't asked to be dragged into this world, hadn't asked for a staff or glowing beasts or a destiny tied to powers she didn't understand. But the image of a Belofez was rising from Miketo's wrath still clung to her thoughts, and her tongue refused to move.

The silence stretched.

Finally, Garantuke exhaled, his shoulders sagging only an inch. "Go. Back to the village. Before you do worse."

He turned from her, but not before she saw it—his eyes, tight with something beyond anger. Fear.

It cut deeper than the shouting had.

By the time they reached Tuspin, word had already outrun them.

Villagers' whispers coiled like smoke as Perrin trudged behind Garantuke, the wooden staff heavy against her shoulder. Children stared from behind root-pillars, eyes wide, while their parents pulled them back. Every face carried the same unspoken judgment: outsider, danger, curse.

Garantuke shoved open the vine-latticed doors of the **Hall of Scrolls**. The air inside was thick with the dry tang of parchment and the low thrum of Miketo woven into the walls. Runes glowed faintly across the roots like veins of fire.

The Elders were waiting. Half a dozen figures, hair braided with threads of light, robes lined with living moss that pulsed faintly in rhythm with their breath. They turned as one, their gazes pinning Perrin like insects on glass.

"She defied our boundary," one said, voice brittle as bark.

"She stirred the Path," another added, glowering at the scorch marks still faint on her sleeve. "Already Miketo trembles."

Perrin hugged the staff closer, wishing it would swallow her whole.

"She should be expelled before she dooms us," said a third.

"Or trained," argued another, her tone sharp. "Better a reckless child under watch than a reckless child abandoned."

Their voices overlapped, rising, falling, like a storm circling the chamber. Perrin stood rooted in the center, cheeks hot, eyes darting from one ancient face to the next. None looked at her like she was a girl—they looked at her like she was a crack in the dam, about to break.

Finally, the eldest Elder—his braid trailing all the way to the floor—raised his hand. The others fell silent.

"Young one," he said, his eyes sharp beneath their heavy lids. "Miketo is not mercy. It is balance. When it is honored, it heals. When it is mocked, it punishes. Do you know what rises when arrogance stirs it?"

Perrin swallowed, throat dry. She thought of the Belofez from the scroll she had been shown earlier, the scaled monstrosity birthed from misuse.

Her silence was answer enough.

"Remember this," the elder said, leaning forward, voice low as stone grinding. "If you disrespect Miketo again, it will not be only you who bleeds. It will be Tuspin. All of us."

The words pressed like chains around her ribs.

Before she could answer, the ground beneath her feet trembled—a faint, warning rumble that silenced even the elders. Dust sifted down from the roots overhead.

The eldest closed his eyes. "Already, it stirs."

The tremor didn't stop.

It deepened, rolling through the Hall of Scrolls until the walls themselves seemed to inhale and exhale with a rhythm not their own. The glow from the runes flickered, shuddering like candlelight in a gale.

Perrin's stomach lurched. She grabbed at her staff for balance, but even it quivered in her grip, humming like it was afraid.

From outside came shouts. The deep blare of horns followed, shaking the cavern air. The villagers' alarm had a sound like no human-made bell—low, bone-rattling, meant to wake even the stone.

Garantuke stiffened beside her. "No..." His voice was

little more than breath, but Perrin caught it.

The eldest elder's face had gone ashen. "The Belofez," he whispered.

The chamber erupted into chaos—elders barking orders, warriors rushing from the hall, villagers' cries rising like surf.

Perrin's pulse pounded so hard it drowned the noise. She had read the word in the scrolls, seen the drawings of creatures too big to be real. But the way fear carved itself into Garantuke's face told her those pictures hadn't been exaggerations.

Her mistake on the Path hadn't just hurt her. It had woken something.

The tremor came again, this time sharper, like claws raking through the bones of the earth. The glow of the runes flared bright, then went dark all at once, plunging the Hall of Scrolls into shadow.

And in that silence—between the horns, between the cries—Perrin thought she heard it.

A hiss. Low, drawn-out. Ancient. Hungry.

It came from below.

CHAPTER 7: A BELOFEZ LIZARD ATTACKS

The ground tore open with a sound like stone screaming.

Perrin staggered against the carved roots of the Hall of Scrolls as the floor heaved beneath her feet. Dust rained from the ceiling, stinging her eyes, and the horns outside blared so loud her bones shook. Villagers sprinted past the doorway, their shouts a wild, panicked chorus.

Then she saw it.

From the far cavern wall, a fissure split wide, vomiting shards of stone and rivers of dirt. Something massive forced its way through, scales grinding against rock, jaws unhinging in a hiss that filled the cavern like steam escaping a kettle.

Its body was long, too long—like a nightmare lizard dragged from some forgotten age. Shards of glass seemed embedded in its hide, glinting with every twitch. When it reared, its tongue lashed out, jagged and serrated, dripping a dark saliva that hissed where it struck stone.

The Belofez.

Perrin froze. She'd seen the horrific sketch in the Hall of Scrolls—inked warnings scrawled by trembling hands centuries ago. But drawings hadn't captured the smell of sulfur and blood that poured from its gullet, or the crushing weight of its presence, like it dragged the whole cavern's air with it.

Villagers armed with staffs and stone-bladed spears shouted to one another, forming a desperate line. Mothers snatched children away, retreating toward the tunnels. The glow of the fungal lights flickered and dimmed, as though even Miketo wanted to hide.

The beast roared again, a sound that sent cracks spidering through the cavern floor.

And Perrin knew—this was no random attack.

It was her fault.

"Hold the line!" Garantuke's voice cut through the chaos like a blade.

He leapt into the clearing, obsidian-plated armor strapped across his shoulders, staff alive with Miketo's glow. The warriors of Tuspin surged with him, their movements sharp and practiced, forming a crescent that flanked the monster.

The Belofez lunged.

Its jaws snapped shut on empty air as Garantuke slid beneath its neck, driving his staff upward. Sparks of Miketo burst from the strike, but did no damage to the beast's scaled hide. It shrieked, staggering back, but not before its serrated tongue lashed out, slicing across a villager's shoulder. Blood spattered the cavern wall.

Then Perrin caught sight of **Selena**. The usually soft-spoken young woman hurled herself into the fight with a wild cry, her staff trailing a sudden violet shimmer. For an instant—just an instant—the purple glow twisted into the shape of a whirlwind, snapping with heat and force, before collapsing back into nothing. The Belofez was flung from the whirlwind, its scales hissing where the purple flame had kissed it, but once again, it took no real damage.

Perrin blinked, breath caught. What had she just seen?

Beside her, **Kimilo** fought with exact precision. Every move was deliberate, measured—the sweep of her staff against the beast's leg, the quick pivot to strike its tail, the way she ducked just before a shard of stone went whistling past her head. She didn't waste energy. Every strike was purposeful, a dance with Miketo instead of a brawl. Kimilo was forcing the beast to use its mouth to attack her while other warriors waited to stab inside its mouth.

Perrin's chest tightened. This was what it looked like to wield Miketo properly—not the reckless flailing she'd tried on the Path, but control. Discipline. Respect.

Garantuke roared, swinging his staff with bone-breaking force. The obsidian weapon connected with the beast's tongue, severing the tip. A spray of dark blood gushed forth, sizzling where it touched the ground. The Belofez shrieked again, retreating a step, its massive body coiling like a serpent preparing to strike anew. The spewing blood became a flood. Perhaps that is where its weakness lay.

The warriors tightened their circle, but the ground trembled with every lash of its tail. Root-bridges snapped, platforms toppled, and entire sections of Tuspin groaned as though the village itself might collapse.

Through it all, Perrin clung to the carved roots of the Hall, powerless to do more than watch.

"Stay here!" one of the guards barked, shoving Perrin back against the carved root wall of the Hall. His voice was rough, but the panic behind it made it clear—keeping her out of the way was as much for the village as for her.

"I can help!" she shouted, heart hammering. The words tasted like desperation.

"No—you'll make it worse." The door slammed, vines weaving tight across the frame as Miketo itself sealed her inside.

Perrin pressed her palms against the glowing roots, but they held firm. She could only peer through the thin slits of light where the vines hadn't fully closed, her view fractured into shifting shards.

Outside, the Belofez roared, the sound so massive it rattled her bones. She glimpsed Garantuke darting beneath its lashing tail, his strikes, like Kimilo's, did no damage, but to force the great lizard to open its mouth, his face set with a determination that made her chest ache. Selena's violet shimmer flickered once, then disappeared again, hidden as quickly as it had come. Kimilo's calm, precise movements threaded through the chaos like a counterpoint to the beast's fury.

And Perrin—she could do nothing.

She slammed her fists against the vine-door until her knuckles stung. She shouted until her throat burned. But the only response was the answering quake of the beast's fury and the villagers' cries of pain. Every bit of the beast's thrashing damaged villagers or property.

Every scream outside sliced through her, sharp and accusing. *This is your fault. You wanted to prove yourself. You brought this.*

Perrin sank to her knees, her forehead against the roots, trying to shut out the sounds of breaking stone and snapping bridges. But they echoed inside her chest as if her ribs were hollow drums.

Helpless. Useless. Watching while others bled.

And the sickening thought gnawed at her: maybe the guard was right. Maybe she really would have only made it worse.

The air inside the Hall quaked with every impact outside. Dust sifted from the high roots overhead, drifting down in glowing motes that clung to Perrin's lashes.

Through the narrow gaps she saw chaos unfolding.

A root-bridge gave way with a shuddering crack,

villagers tumbling as the living vines recoiled from the Belofez's weight. Warriors scrambled to haul the fallen back up before the beast's jaws could snap them in two. Blood gleamed like spilled ink on the glowing floor, too much of it pooling near the Healing Hall's entrance.

The Belofez lashed its severed tongue like a whip, spraying dark blood across the stone. Where the droplets landed, the roots hissed and shriveled, their glow flickering as if life itself recoiled.

Perrin's stomach twisted. She pressed her fist against her mouth to hold back a sob.

A woman staggered into view, clutching a child to her chest. One of the beast's claws swept through the space she had just occupied, slicing deep furrows into the stone wall. She would have been crushed if not for Kimilo—calm, unshaken—darting forward to drag her to safety with one arm while striking the claw aside with her staff.

Selena appeared next, eyes wild, lips pulled back in a soundless cry as she slammed her staff against the beast's side. The faintest pulse of violet wind rippled out, toppling debris, pushing the creature back for a heartbeat.

Garantuke fought at the front, his strikes raining down with a fury Perrin had never seen in him before. He wasn't just defending—he was punishing, driving the beast away from the wounded, his every movement daring it to face him instead of the helpless.

But still it wasn't enough. Warriors fell. Roofs caved.

The cavern lights dimmed as Tuspin bled.

Perrin's nails dug into her palms. Every instinct screamed to break through the vines, to fling herself into the chaos, to prove she wasn't the useless outsider they thought she was. But the vines pulsed harder under her hands, holding her in place as though Miketo itself had decided she must watch.

And watching was worse than any wound.

When the roar finally fell silent and the cavern stopped shaking, Perrin pressed her face to the vine-slit, desperate to see.

Smoke and dust choked the air outside. The Belofez's body lay in ruin at the edge of the glowing river, its glassy scales still intact, its tongue severed and still twitching in the dirt. Warriors staggered among the wreckage, dragging the injured toward the Healing Hall. Cries of pain mingled with the hiss of water poured over burning vines.

The roots across the doorway loosened at last. Perrin shoved through before they were fully open, stumbling into the ruined square.

Her boots squelched in blood and ash. The sight of shattered homes made her throat ache. Every face she passed twisted in a mix of exhaustion, pain, and something sharper—blame.

Garantuke stood in the center, chest heaving, obsidian staff cracked at the edge from the force of his strikes. His hair clung damp to his brow, his arms streaked with cuts that glowed faintly where Miketo had sealed them halfway shut.

When his gaze found her, Perrin wished the vines had kept her locked away forever.

"You," he rasped, voice raw from shouting commands. He strode toward her, every step heavy with restrained rage. "This happened because of you."

Perrin's mouth opened, closed. "I—I didn't mean—"

"You think meaning matters?" His voice cut sharper than his staff. He jabbed the broken end toward the devastation. "Look at them. Look at what your recklessness brought here."

"I only wanted to help—" she whispered, the words trembling out like smoke.

"Help?" His laugh was bitter, hollow. "If this is help, then may the earth never see your harm." His eyes burned, not just with anger, but with something that pierced deeper—fear. "You could doom us all, Perrin Roberts."

The weight of his words slammed into her harder than the Belofez's roar. Around them, villagers turned away, their murmurs rising again—reckless, cursed, outsider.

Perrin hugged her arms around herself, wishing she could shrink small enough to vanish into the glowing cracks of the cavern floor.

Perrin stayed rooted to the spot long after Garantuke turned his back, shame burning hot in her chest. Around her, the villagers worked in grim silence—binding wounds, clearing rubble, dousing the last smoldering vines. No one looked at her directly, but she could feel their glances, sharp as thrown stones.

A hand brushed her elbow. Selena's face, pale and drawn, met hers. Strands of hair clung to her damp temples, and her eyes shimmered with something Perrin couldn't place—fear, maybe, or grief.

"You saw it," Selena murmured, voice pitched low. "The violet wind."

Perrin blinked, remembering the violent rush that had blasted the Belofez sideways, scattering debris. "That was... you?"

Selena shook her head quickly, eyes darting to the elders across the square. "Not now. Not here. Just—don't hate me for it."

"Hate you? You saved them." Perrin's voice cracked.

Selena's throat worked, but she said no more. Her hand lingered on Perrin's sleeve for a heartbeat, then fell away, retreating like a secret she wasn't ready to share.

Kimilo appeared next, her calm presence a strange balm amid the wreckage. She crouched to help a boy with a split shoulder, her hands steady as she wrapped a strip of glowing moss around the wound. The child whimpered once, then went still as the light seeped into his skin.

"You can't force Miketo," Kimilo said softly, not looking up. "It doesn't follow hunger. It follows need. Tonight, you learned the difference."

Perrin's face heated. She wanted to argue, to say she hadn't asked for this, that none of this was fair. But the words dried on her tongue.

Her gaze slipped to Garantuke. He stood with the warriors, barking orders as they dragged the Belofez's carcass toward the cavern's edge. His shoulders were rigid with exhaustion, but still he held himself like a wall, daring the world to strike again.

Perrin's chest ached. Anger, shame, and something far more complicated tangled inside her. She hated how badly she wanted him to look at her—not with fury, but with the same steadiness he gave the others.

Instead, she stood small in the glow of broken vines, swallowing the weight of everything she'd done.

The cavern grew quiet again, the silence heavy and uneven, broken only by the scrape of shovels and the distant hiss of water running through the roots. The Belofez was gone, dragged into the abyss, but its presence lingered like a bruise on the whole village.

Perrin stood apart, her hands balled into fists at her sides. She could still feel the way the vines had wrapped around her, locking her away, shutting her out as if she were the threat. Maybe she was.

Her gaze dropped to the faintly glowing staff at her feet. Its surface pulsed once, a slow thrum that felt almost like a heartbeat. Perrin bent to pick it up. This time, instead of clenching it like a weapon, she cradled it in both hands.

"I get it," she whispered, though her throat was tight. "I can't just... grab power because I want it. I see what happens when I do." Her eyes stung. "I don't want to be the reason they bleed. Not again."

The staff pulsed warmer, almost approving.

Perrin lifted her chin, squaring her shoulders. For the first time since falling into this world, she didn't feel like running or proving or shouting. She only felt the weight of what she had to learn.

"I'll listen," she said, more firmly this time. "I'll wait. I'll do it right."

From across the square, Garantuke glanced at her, his expression unreadable, but something in his gaze—less fury, more consideration—anchored her vow.

Perrin pressed the staff against her chest, the glow seeping through her fingers. She didn't know what respecting Miketo really meant yet, but she knew this much: it was the only way forward.

CHAPTER 8: THE GIFT OF MIKETO

The morning air in Tuspin felt different after the Belofez attack—cooler, sharper, as if even the glowing roots that lined the cavern walls were waiting to see whether she'd blunder again. Perrin clutched her staff with both hands, its weight both reassuring and accusing, and tried not to let her knees knock together.

The training grounds were a wide circle of smooth stone, etched with runes that glowed faintly when anyone stepped inside. She hated how exposed it felt. No crowds of schoolmates this time, no cameras recording her next mistake—but the villagers' silent stares cut sharper than any phone screen ever had.

Selena stood off to one side, her straight black hair braided close against her head, her eyes watchful. Kimilo, slight and precise, tied her black hair into a knot and rolled her shoulders like someone about to correct Perrin's every move. Garantuke was already inside the circle, tall and steady, his arms folded. His expression gave nothing away, but the memory of his fury the night before still burned in Perrin's chest.

She swallowed hard and stepped into the circle. The runes brightened under her shoes, a pulse of energy running up her ankles. She almost flinched.

"You don't have to be afraid of it," Garantuke said, his voice even but not unkind. "You only have to respect it."

"I'm not afraid," Perrin lied. Her grip tightened until her knuckles ached.

"Then show us," Kimilo said, bowing slightly before stepping back.

Selena offered a gentler smile. "Start simple. Breathe first."

Perrin drew in air that smelled faintly of damp stone and glowing moss, held it, and tried to quiet the clamor in her head. She wasn't Perrin the punchline anymore. Not here. If she messed this up, there were no second takes, no delete buttons—only real consequences.

Her staff warmed in her hands as if listening. She exhaled, squared her shoulders, and nodded once.

"All right," she muttered. "Round two."

Selena stepped into the circle first, her presence like a calming tide. She lifted her own staff—dark wood veined with a faint violet glow—and showed Perrin a basic stance. "Feet apart, not too wide. One steady, one free. Think of balance before power."

Perrin tried to mimic her, but her staff wobbled, the tip clacking against the stone. She winced.

"Too tight," Selena said softly. She touched Perrin's

hands, easing her grip until it felt almost wrong. "Let the staff listen to you. It doesn't need to be strangled."

"Tell that to my nerves," Perrin muttered.

Selena chuckled. "Nerves mean you care. Good. Keep them."

Kimilo moved in next, her steps quick and exact, her own slender staff flicking in sharp arcs. Where Selena's style was fluid, Kimilo's was crisp, every strike cutting the air with surgical precision. "Miketo is energy," she explained, her Japanese accent giving the words a clipped music. "If you scatter your thoughts, it scatters too. Be clean. Be sharp."

She lunged suddenly. Perrin yelped and barely managed to block. The clash rattled her arms all the way to her shoulders.

"Again," Kimilo said, already swinging.

This time Perrin braced, remembering Selena's balance and Kimilo's sharpness. She caught the strike better, though her knees still buckled.

Kimilo's eyes narrowed, but not cruelly. "Better."

By the third exchange, Perrin found herself laughing —half with relief, half with nerves. Selena smiled at the sound. Kimilo only grunted approval, which for her was practically applause.

For the first time since falling into this world, Perrin felt the faintest thread of belonging tugging at her chest. She wasn't good yet. She wasn't even close. But standing between Selena's grace and Kimilo's precision, she could almost imagine herself learning how not to mess everything up.

The training circle emptied slowly, villagers drifting back to their work, but Garantuke stayed. He leaned his staff across his shoulders and watched Perrin until she squirmed.

"What?" she asked, still catching her breath.

"You laugh too easily," he said, not unkindly. "But maybe that's better than silence."

She tilted her head. "You say that like it's a bad thing."

"It can be. Laughter makes you light. But light things are easy to break." His gaze drifted past her, far beyond the cavern walls, to a place she couldn't see. The weight of it pulled the air taut between them.

Perrin's voice softened. "You've lost someone."

He didn't answer at first. His jaw flexed, then loosened. Finally, he lowered his staff and planted it in the ground, leaning on it like a confession.

"My father," he said. Just two words, but they seemed to echo through the cavern. "He stood against Malum when he first set foot in Tuspin to steal the Star-Stone, our village's treasure. It fell from the sky, shot through the earth, and landed on the pinnacle of the Hall of Scrolls. The villagers thought it beautiful, but then we found some power inside that protected us from the Belofez and enlightened our minds. My father thought strength would be enough to stop Malum from taking it. It wasn't."

Perrin's throat tightened. "I'm sorry."

"He was stronger than me. Wiser. But Malum's voice..." He looked at her then, sharp and searching, as if he were measuring her against a memory. "It rots a man from the inside. My father struck once, then twice, and then—" His hand clenched the staff until his knuckles whitened. "And then he struck me. His own son. Malum had hollowed him out that quickly."

Perrin's breath caught. She wanted to say something— anything—but the words tangled in her chest.

Garantuke looked away. "I buried what was left of him with my own hands. The stone that marks his grave still remembers by glowing brightly both night and day. That's why I fight as I do. Not for myself. For him. For all who could not resist."

The silence that followed wasn't empty. It was full—of grief, of promise, of something Perrin didn't know how to carry.

She finally whispered, "Then I'll fight too. For him."

Garantuke's eyes flicked back to hers. For a heartbeat, something softened there, like a crack in armor. Then it was gone, sealed behind duty once more.

After Garantuke's words, the training ground felt heavier, like the air itself was listening. Perrin tried not to fidget, but her palms itched for something to do. She let her gaze wander across the cavern floor, tracing the cracks in the stone, the stray glimmers of fungus light.

That's when she saw it.

Half-buried near the edge of the ring, a shard caught the glow — not like the green of the roots or the silver-white of the fungi, but a flicker of blue. Deep, rich, alive. She crouched before she thought better of it, brushing the dirt aside with quick, nervous fingers.

The shard wasn't just stone. It looked like metal, but not any kind she'd ever seen. Its surface shimmered as though it held a river under glass. Veins of light pulsed faintly through it, like it had a heartbeat of its own.

"What's this?" she whispered, reaching for it.

The instant her fingers closed around it, a jolt ran up her arm — not sharp, but insistent, like the air pressing into her skin. She gasped and nearly dropped it, but the shard clung to her palm as if it had chosen her.

Garantuke's voice cut across the circle. "Don't touch that."

Too late. Perrin staggered upright, the blue-stone still glowing in her hand. "It—it won't let go."

Villagers at the edges froze. Selena's mouth parted in shock, while Kimilo took a sharp step forward, eyes wide. A low murmur spread through the cavern, suspicion and awe tangled together.

The shard pulsed again, brighter this time, and Perrin's skin prickled as if every nerve in her hand had been rewired. She swallowed hard, trying not to look terrified.

"I didn't mean—" Her voice wavered. "I just found it."

But even as she said it, a strange certainty curled in her chest. The shard hadn't been lost. It had been waiting.

The shard throbbed against her palm, heat rising until Perrin hissed and tried to fling it away. But it didn't fall. Instead, the blue veins flared and spilled light up her arm, winding like a living braid.

"Drop it!" Garantuke barked, moving toward her.

"I can't!" Perrin's voice cracked. She clutched her wrist with her free hand, as if she could stop the current running through her.

The ground beneath her feet trembled faintly, not like the dangerous quake of the Belofez but something subtler —like roots adjusting themselves, listening. The villagers drew back instinctively.

Selena whispered, "It's choosing."

The shard softened in her grip. No—that wasn't right. It stretched, lengthened, reshaped itself as though melted and pulled by invisible hands. Perrin watched in horror and awe as the glowing metal elongated into a staff the height of her shoulder, ridged with veins of light, its surface rough as bark in some places, smooth as water-polished stone in others. And in some places, clear as if it were glass.

When the light finally dimmed, Perrin staggered back, clutching the new weapon. It was lighter than she expected—perfectly balanced, like it had been made for her.

"It's... mine?" she whispered, almost afraid of the word.

"No," Kimilo said firmly, her dark eyes steady. "It is

Miketo's. It only lets you carry it."

The villagers erupted into debate—some crossing themselves in gestures of warding, others leaning forward in reverent awe. A girl from the far edge hissed, "She doesn't deserve it," while an old man muttered, "No outsider has ever..."

Garantuke silenced them with a raised hand, but his gaze was fixed on Perrin, unreadable. "Miketo has spoken."

The words dropped heavy into the cavern.

Perrin gripped the staff tighter. She hadn't earned this. She knew it. And yet—the staff's faint hum ran through her skin like a heartbeat that wasn't hers, binding her to it whether she wanted it or not.

That night, Perrin couldn't sleep.

Tuspin's cavern always hummed faintly, like the world itself was breathing, but now the sound wove around her differently. She lay on her woven mat in the dim chamber given to her, the new staff propped against the wall within arm's reach. Its surface caught the glow of the fungus-lamps, veins of blue faintly alive even in rest.

She told herself not to look at it. That if she ignored it, maybe she could pretend it wasn't there, that she wasn't now responsible for something she barely understood.

But her eyes kept sliding back.

When she finally gave in and reached for it, her fingers brushed the staff's ridged surface. The pulse came instantly, climbing up her arm. Not pain. Not comfort.

Something in between, like being stared at by the night sky itself.

And then— Not words. Impressions. Echoes inside her head.

Shadow awaits. Sacred Blood. Graywun's line bends but does not break.

Perrin gasped, yanking her hand back. Her heart rattled in her chest like it wanted out.

"Hello?" she whispered to the empty chamber, half-hoping it was Selena or Kimilo playing a trick. Nothing answered—except the staff, humming faintly again, as though it had enjoyed her fear.

She pressed her palms over her ears, squeezing her eyes shut. "Stop. Just stop."

The whispers faded, but the hum lingered—constant, insistent, like it was waiting for her to ask another question.

And the worst part was... some small, traitorous part of her wanted to.

The chamber chilled suddenly, though no draft stirred the hanging moss at the entry. Perrin's breath misted. She clutched the staff tighter, its glow dimming as though it too had gone still.

A shape wavered near the corner, tall and half-transparent until it thickened into form. Moonshadow stepped from nothing, her skin the soft hue of twilight blue, her eyes silvered like water under stars. She carried no sound with her, only the pressure of presence, as if the whole cavern bent inward to make room for her.

Perrin scrambled to her feet, pulse banging against her ribs. "You—" Her voice cracked. "You said Eric was Malum. That he—he *made* me—"

Moonshadow's gaze cut her off. Calm. Unyielding. She looked at the staff, then back at Perrin. "You should not have it yet."

"It chose me," Perrin shot back, defensive despite herself. "It gave itself to me."

The woman tilted her head, braid of dark hair falling like a pendulum. "Miketo does not give. It tests. And every gift has a cost."

Perrin's throat went dry. She thought of the whispers. *Shadow awaits. Sacred Blood. Graywun's line bends but does not break.* "What kind of cost?"

Moonshadow stepped closer, her bare feet silent on the woven mat. "The same cost your grandmother paid when she bore her name, Graywun. The same cost your mother carries every day and does not speak of. Knowledge. Burden. Sacrifice."

The words landed heavy, each one a stone Perrin didn't know how to hold.

Moonshadow's voice softened, though it still thrummed with otherworldly weight. "Listen well: Eric is not merely a boy with a voice that bends weak wills. He is Malum, the corrupter. He has tasted Miketo before, and he will devour it again if given the chance. If you walk foolishly, you will feed him."

Perrin gripped the staff harder, knuckles white. "So what do I do? Just... give up? Run?"

Moonshadow's expression didn't change, but her eyes deepened, like looking into a pool too dark to see the bottom. "You learn. You respect. And you wait until you are more than the child he believes you to be."

And just like that, the cold lifted. Moonshadow dissolved into the cavern air, leaving only the dim pulse of the staff and Perrin's ragged breathing.

She sank to the mat, pressing the staff across her lap. Her stomach twisted between defiance and fear.

"More than a child," she whispered into the dark. "Then I'll make him see it."

The cavern was quiet again, but Perrin couldn't shake the echo of Moonshadow's words. Her fingers traced the length of the staff as if it might explain itself, but all she felt was its steady hum, like a living heartbeat pressed against her palms.

It should have reassured her. Instead, it felt like holding lightning in a bottle—power that wasn't really hers, not yet.

She stood, testing its weight. The blue stone caught the faint glow from the fungi overhead, throwing streaks of light against the walls. For a moment she imagined herself tall and fierce, staff raised, every villager bowing in respect.

But then her grip faltered, and the staff slipped, clattering against the mat with a sound that made her wince. She wasn't fierce. Not yet. She was still the girl who tripped over sprinklers and gave away car keys because someone smiled at her.

Her throat tightened. She bent, scooped the staff back into her hands, and forced herself to breathe evenly.

Behind her, footsteps approached—the soft tread of Selena, Kimilo, and then heavier ones she knew too well. Perrin didn't turn, afraid they'd see the flush on her face, the doubt she couldn't hide.

Garantuke's voice rumbled low. "It is yours now."

She glanced over her shoulder. He stood at the edge of the training space, arms folded, eyes unreadable. His presence steadied her and unsettled her at once.

"I don't know how to use it," she admitted.

"You will learn," Kimilo said simply, as if it were fact.

Selena offered a small, encouraging smile, though her gaze flicked nervously toward Garantuke. "Miketo doesn't choose lightly."

Perrin hugged the staff closer. She wanted to believe them. She *needed* to.

But deep down she knew the truth: the staff had chosen her, yes—but that didn't mean she was ready for what came next.

And somewhere beyond the cavern walls, in the dark places where Eric—no, Malum—waited, she swore she could feel a faint tug, like invisible fingers plucking at the same thread of energy now bound to her.

The staff pulsed once, sharp and hot in her hands, as if

to remind her: *This is only the beginning.*

CHAPTER 9: LOVE AND JEALOUSY

The training circle shimmered again with its faint runes, the air thrumming like a low drumbeat under Perrin's boots. She twirled her staff, trying to mimic Selena's fluidity and Kimilo's precision—but every time Garantuke stepped closer, her grip slipped just a little.

"Focus," he said, circling her like a hawk. His tone was steady, but his eyes tracked her every movement.

"I *am* focusing," she shot back, spinning her staff too fast. The tip clanged against the stone, sparks skipping. Her face flushed.

Garantuke reached forward, closing his hand gently over hers. He steadied the staff, tilting it to the proper angle. His fingers were rough, callused from years of training, and the heat of his skin shot up her arm faster than Miketo's energy ever had.

Her heart hammered. *Focus, Perrin. Not on him. On the staff.*

"Your stance is wrong," he said, his voice low. He stepped behind her, nudging her feet apart with the side of his boot. His nearness made the cavern shrink, every breath of air charged.

She swallowed hard. "Better?"

"Yes. If you hold still for once."

She forced her knees to bend, staff braced the way he'd shown. When he pressed lightly against her back, urging her to straighten her shoulders, she nearly forgot to breathe. The runes underfoot flared brighter, picking up her pulse.

For a heartbeat, neither of them moved. His hand lingered a fraction too long on the staff, his breath ghosting close enough to stir the fine hairs at her temple. Perrin's chest ached with the confusing thrill of it—half fear, half something else she didn't have a name for yet.

Then he stepped back, the moment snapping like a string pulled too tight. "Again," he said, all duty once more.

But Perrin couldn't shake the warmth that clung to her skin where his hand had been.

They sparred until Perrin's arms ached, until her staff felt heavier than the day she first picked it up. Sweat stung her eyes, but she refused to quit—not while Garantuke watched her like every slip might be her last.

She lunged one final time, their staffs clashing with a sharp crack that echoed through the cavern. He twisted easily, disarming her. Her staff clattered across the stone, skidding to a stop at the edge of the circle.

Perrin froze, chest heaving. Garantuke stood a breath

away, his own staff angled at her chest. For a long moment, neither moved.

Then his weapon dropped. He reached out—not to strike, but to steady her shoulder. His palm lingered there, warm, grounding.

"You're reckless," he said, softer now. "But you're learning."

Her throat tightened. She wanted to look away, but his eyes held her still, the faint glow of the cavern lights reflecting in them.

"I don't know how to stop being reckless," she admitted. The words tumbled out before she could think. "It's like... if I don't act, if I don't *do* something, then I'll never matter. I'll always be the stupid girl who posts at the wrong time and ruins everything."

His hand slid from her shoulder to her wrist, lifting it gently, as though reminding her she still held power. "You matter here."

Her breath hitched. The air between them vibrated with something more dangerous than any Miketo strike.

"I shouldn't," she whispered. "You said I could doom you all."

"And yet," he said, stepping closer, his voice dropping to a near-growl, "I don't want you gone."

The words cracked something in her chest. Before she could second-guess herself, Perrin blurted, "I like you."

His grip tightened—just enough to let her feel it. "I know." A faint smile ghosted across his lips. "And I like you too."

The confession hung there, fragile and burning, a truth neither of them could take back.

For a moment after their confession, silence held them. The only sounds were the faint drip of water from the cavern roof and the echo of Perrin's too-fast heartbeat.

She wanted to keep the moment alive, to stretch it into forever. Instead, words spilled out—messy, impulsive, the way they always did with her.

"You could come with me," she blurted.

Garantuke blinked. "Come with you?"

"When I get back home. Arizona." Her voice sped up, nervous. "It's not all desert and heat, you know. There are mountains, and saguaros, and places where the stars go on forever. My mom would... well, she'd probably freak out at first, but she'd get used to you. Maybe." She tried for a smile, but it faltered. "You don't have to stay buried down here. You could have a life. With me."

For half a heartbeat, she thought he might say yes. His expression softened, his lips parted—then he closed them again, the shift so sharp it made her stomach drop.

"I can't," he said firmly.

"Can't?"

"My place is here. Tuspin needs me. The roots need me. If I leave, I abandon what my father died protecting." His jaw tightened, his eyes dark. "You ask me to betray him."

Perrin's chest hollowed. "I wasn't asking you to betray him. I was asking you to... choose me." The last words came out small, almost swallowed.

He shook his head, stepping back. "You don't understand. Not yet."

The warmth of their confession cooled into a heavy silence. Perrin clutched her staff, wishing she could take the words back—or twist them into something better. But she couldn't.

All she could feel was the sting of rejection curling through her chest, sharp and hot.

Later that day, Perrin wandered the village paths, still raw from their conversation. The glow of the roots felt dimmer than usual, and every villager's glance seemed sharper, as if they all knew she'd just been told no.

She found herself near the market clearing, where baskets of fruit glistened with dew and giant butterflies drifted lazily above the stalls. Voices carried—laughter, light and familiar. She followed the sound before she realized what she was doing.

Garantuke stood near one of the root-bridges, speaking with a girl about Perrin's age. The girl's hair was dark like his, her eyes bright. When she smiled, it lit the whole space around her.

Perrin froze as Garantuke reached out, pulling the girl into a hug. Not a casual embrace, either—his arms wrapped strong around her shoulders, his face buried briefly in her hair as she laughed softly.

The sight punched through Perrin's chest like a staff strike.

Her stomach churned. *So that's why he won't leave Tuspin. Not because of duty. Because of her.*

Heat swelled behind her eyes. She stumbled back, heart pounding, breath shallow. Every laugh from the girl, every curve of Garantuke's smile, pressed tighter against her ribs until she thought she might explode.

She didn't wait to hear another word. Spinning on her heel, Perrin bolted toward the cavern's edge, clutching her staff like it was the only thing still hers.

And deep inside, a whisper unfurled—jealous, reckless, dangerous. *I'll show him. I don't need him.*

Perrin's boots slapped against the cavern stone, her breath coming fast and jagged. She didn't care where she was going—anywhere away from that hug, from the laughter that kept replaying in her skull.

She followed a narrow path twisting between roots that glowed faintly blue, leading toward the darker reaches of Tuspin's edge. The air grew colder, quieter, as though even the cavern wanted her gone.

"Stupid," she muttered, swiping angrily at her face. "He says it's duty. But it's her. Always her. I should've known."

A rustle broke the silence. Then a second.

Perrin froze, her grip tightening on the staff. Shadows detached from the wall, reshaping into tall, thin figures in beige vests and top hats, their boots clacking backward against the stone.

Contrary Men.

Their faces were pale, eyes unfocused, lips curling in warped smiles. One of them tipped his hat—backward, of course—and opened his mouth.

"Y-lla-e-r," the words tumbled out in reverse, garbled and fast.

Perrin's skin crawled. "I don't... I don't know what you're saying."

Another snapped his fingers, and a glowing sphere of energy flared to life, spinning in his palm. The hum of it set her teeth on edge.

Her heart leapt into her throat, but she forced her staff up. "Fine. You want to fight? Then fight."

The Contrary Men circled her in jagged steps, their laughter pitched high and wrong. The first sphere shot forward, slamming into the stone near her feet. Heat blasted up her legs, leaving her stumbling.

Her pulse surged. Miketo's energy stirred, alive in her staff, ready to answer her fury.

She squared her shoulders, breath shaking. "I'm not scared of you."

But the quiver in her voice betrayed her.

The first sphere had barely faded before another came, whistling past Perrin's shoulder. She ducked, fury spiking hotter than fear. The runes in her staff flared, alive to her anger.

"Not this time," she snarled.

She swung hard, pouring everything into the strike. Blue light ripped from the staff, a raw surge that blasted outward in a crackling arc. The Contrary Men staggered back, their backward steps faltering, hats flying askew.

For a heartbeat, Perrin thrilled at the sight—*finally*, she was strong, finally she was winning.

Then the arc didn't stop.

It whipped wild across the cavern, striking a root wall and splitting it with a thunderous crack. Shards of glowing bark flew. The light rebounded, spiraling back toward her like a living whip.

"Perrin!"

Garantuke's voice cut through the chaos just as he burst into the clearing, staff raised.

Too late. The wild surge veered toward him.

"No!" Perrin screamed. She twisted her staff, trying to reel the power back, but it fought her, slippery and untamed. The wave of blue light slammed into Garantuke's left side, knocking him off his feet. He hit the ground hard, his staff clattering away.

The Contrary Men cackled, words spilling backward, gleeful at the spectacle.

Perrin's blood iced. She hadn't just failed—she'd nearly destroyed the one person who still believed she *might* belong here.

The laughter of the Contrary Men swelled, high and broken, echoing off the cavern walls. Perrin stumbled toward Garantuke, her staff trembling in her grip. He was on one knee, clutching his ribs, his face pale in the glow.

"I didn't— I didn't mean—" The words tangled in her

throat, useless.

Before the Contrary Men could close in, horns sounded in the distance—short, sharp blasts that made the air itself vibrate.

From the shadows, Tuspin's patrol burst forth. Warriors in dark armor of root-woven plates surged into the fray, staffs spinning with trained precision. The cavern erupted into flashes of light and pounding strikes.

One Contrary Man hurled a sphere of energy, only to have it sliced in half mid-air by a glowing arc from Kimilo. Selena followed, her movements fluid as water, scattering the enemy with controlled gusts of Miketo.

The rest of the patrol pressed forward, forcing the twisted men back step by backward step until they melted into the dark with jeering laughter, their top hats bobbing one last time before vanishing.

Perrin dropped to her knees beside Garantuke. His breath came ragged, his hand still pressed to his side where her strike had landed.

"I hurt you," she whispered, horror prickling up her arms.

His eyes met hers, sharp with pain but steady. "Not... as badly as you hurt yourself."

Her chest constricted. Around them, the patrol regrouped, Selena and Kimilo flanking her with guarded looks—not of comfort this time, but of judgment.

The weight of what she'd done settled heavy on her shoulders.

The walk back to Tuspin was silent except for the faint clink of weapons and the rasp of Garantuke's breathing. Perrin trailed at the center of the patrol, staff dragging against the stone as if it, too, judged her.

When they reached the village square, horns sounded again—this time not for battle, but for summons. Elders filed into the Hall of Scrolls, their robes brushing the floor, faces lit by the shifting glow of root-light.

Perrin stood before them, every villager watching from the shadows. Garantuke leaned heavily on another warrior, refusing to sit despite his injury. His silence burned worse than any shouted anger.

One elder's voice cracked like brittle wood. "Twice you have brought peril to Tuspin."

"She nearly struck down Garantuke," another hissed. "Were it not for the patrol—"

"She cannot remain free," a third said, eyes narrow. "Recklessness draws doom."

Perrin's stomach twisted. She wanted to argue, to scream that she hadn't meant it, that she'd only wanted to prove herself. But the words withered under their gazes. She had no defense.

The eldest elder raised a hand, silencing the chamber. His voice was low, final. "Until discipline tempers her, she is confined. She shall not train. She shall not wander. She will learn patience in solitude, or she will be cast out."

Gasps rippled through the villagers.

Perrin's chest hollowed. Confined. Alone. The one

punishment she couldn't spin into defiance.

Warriors stepped forward. Selena's gaze softened as if she wanted to speak, but Kimilo's jaw tightened, keeping her silent. Garantuke looked away.

The staff pulsed once in Perrin's hands, faint but insistent—like it, too, disagreed.

But no one else did.

They led her to a small stone chamber carved into the roots beneath the Hall. No windows, just the steady glow of fungi on the walls. The door shut with a dull thud, and the lock slid into place.

Perrin slumped against the wall, the weight of her staff across her knees. It pulsed once, then stilled, as though even Miketo had grown weary of her mistakes.

Her thoughts tangled in circles: Garantuke's steady eyes, the girl's smile, the pull in her chest that had driven her to lash out. She had wanted him to choose her; to prove she wasn't just a foolish outsider. Instead, she had nearly destroyed him.

A sick realization crept in, chilling her blood.

This—this was exactly what Eric did. He bent people with his voice, pushed them into choices they wouldn't have made, made them believe lies. And she had done the same thing to herself. She had let her jealousy twist her until her staff struck blindly, hurting the one person she wanted to protect.

Her whisper filled the chamber, rough and trembling: "I'm no better than him."

The staff flickered faintly, almost in denial. But Perrin pressed her forehead to its smooth surface, shame burning behind her eyes.

Jealousy wasn't just childish or petty. It was dangerous. It could hollow her out, just like Eric's voice hollowed her, just like it had hollowed Garantuke's father.

She curled tighter against the wall, clutching the staff like it might keep her anchored.

"I won't let it," she whispered. "I won't be like him."

But even as she said it, she wasn't sure if she believed herself.

CHAPTER 10: THE PUNISHMENT

"Let me out!" Her voice cracked, echoing down the hollow chamber. No answer. Only the steady drip of water from somewhere in the rock above, mocking her with its patience.

She pounded her fists once, twice—then slumped back, the fight bleeding out of her. A single torch fungus glowed on the wall, painting everything in sickly silver light. Her staff leaned in the corner where they'd let her keep it, but only because Miketo itself had flared when a guard had come and tried to take it. Otherwise, she would've been stripped of even that.

The chamber was barely wider than her bedroom closet back home. The air pressed close, heavy with damp earth and the faint tang of root-sap. No sound of the village reached her here. No laughter. No life. Just silence, thick and punishing.

Perrin slid down the wall until she sat on the cold stone, arms wrapped tight around her knees. The punishment wasn't bruises or chains. It was worse: no training. No proving herself. No way to claw back the trust she'd shattered.

Her breath came shallow. She hated stillness. Hated being trapped with nothing but her own thoughts. They twisted sharper than any of the Contrary Men's energy spheres, stabbing her again and again with the memory of Garantuke's face when she struck him.

She whispered into the silence, "I'm not cut out for this place. Maybe they should've left me in the shaft."

The torch fungus dimmed for a heartbeat, as if even it judged her.

The next day, footsteps echoed beyond the door. Perrin scrambled up, hope clawing through her chest. "Garantuke?"

She pressed her ear to the roots, straining. Voices murmured, muffled but sharp. One she recognized instantly—low, steady, edged with steel. It was him.

"...let me through," he demanded.

A second voice cut him off—an elder's, brittle as cracked bark. "No. The council's word was clear. She is to remain in confinement. You will not see her."

Perrin's palms flattened against the barrier. "I'm here!" she shouted. "Please, just let me talk to him!"

The voices hushed. For a heartbeat, she thought they might give in. Then the elder's tone rose, final. "You risk undermining the punishment. Do you defy us, Garantuke?"

A pause. Long. Heavy. Perrin held her breath.

When Garantuke spoke again, his voice was quieter, thick with something she couldn't name. "No. I obey."

His footsteps retreated, steady but slow, like each step dragged a weight.

Perrin's chest caved. She sank back onto the floor, her throat aching as if she'd swallowed stone. He hadn't fought harder. He hadn't broken the rules for her. He'd left.

Tears burned her eyes, but she bit them back. Crying wouldn't change anything. Crying wouldn't make him stay.

But the sound of his retreating steps echoed long after silence returned, louder than any accusation the elders had thrown at her.

Days blurred together. Perrin lost track of how long she'd been locked away, measuring time only by the dimming and brightening of the torch fungi. The stillness pressed in until even her thoughts felt loud.

Sometimes, the guards allowed her a narrow slit of vision through the woven roots of an adjacent room. Just enough to remind her what she was missing.

From there, she watched the village repair the damage the Belofez had left behind. Roots were coaxed into new bridges, their glowing strands woven by practiced hands. Families hauled rubble, humming in rhythm as they stacked stones into walls. Selena guided children away from the dangerous edges while Kimilo worked side by side with elders, her movements sharp and purposeful.

And Garantuke—always in the center of it. Directing, lifting, fighting through the pain of his half-healed ribs. He never looked toward her cell, not once, though Perrin searched his face every time.

The more she watched, the heavier her chest grew. These people bled for each other. They didn't need a foolish outsider stumbling into their world, breaking more than she fixed.

When a child ran past her view carrying a basket bigger than their head, Perrin's throat clenched. She should've been out there helping. She should've been training harder, fighting harder, *being* better. Instead, her selfishness had left her locked away while everyone else rebuilt what she had endangered.

Her reflection wavered faintly in the glowing roots. The face staring back wasn't the one she wanted to see—it was smaller, weaker, shadowed by guilt.

She whispered to it, voice raw, "You ruin everything. Just like always."

The roots didn't answer. They just pulsed once, faintly, as if in agreement.

That night, the silence pressed thicker than ever. Perrin lay curled on the stone, her staff resting against the wall beside her. She tried to sleep, but her mind replayed the elders' judgment, the sight of Garantuke turning away, the sound of laughter cut short by her wild strike.

She groaned, dragging the staff closer as though its weight might ground her.

The moment her fingers brushed the smooth ridges, the hum began again—low and insistent, curling through her skin. She stiffened.

Then the whisper came.

Granddaughter of Graywun.

Perrin jerked, staring around the chamber. No one. Just her and the staff.

The voice wasn't sound. It was inside her, threading through her thoughts.

The shadow waits. The blood remembers the generations before. Only one path opens the way.

Her heart thudded. She gripped the staff tighter. "What does that even mean?" she whispered. "Talk normal, why can't you just talk normal?"

The hum swelled, almost amused. Then—

You are not ready. But you must be.

Perrin pressed her forehead to the staff, eyes squeezed shut. The words twisted like thorns inside her chest. Not ready—but must be. Always too reckless, too jealous, too weak. And yet Miketo, for some reason, hadn't let go of her.

"Why me?" she whispered into the stone-cold silence.

The staff gave no answer. Only another faint pulse, steady as a heartbeat, as if it expected her to figure it out alone.

The rumble woke her before the horns.

Stone dust sifted down from the ceiling as the chamber shuddered. Perrin scrambled upright, clutching her staff. The air outside filled with shouts, then the piercing cry of horns splitting the cavern's stillness.

Her pulse spiked. She knew that sound now—warning. Belofez.

She rushed to the woven roots blocking her door, pressing her face against the small slit. At first she saw only shadows rushing past. Then the beast surged into view.

Even bigger than the last. Its glassy scales glimmered with fractured light, its tongue lashing out like a blade. Every time it hissed, sparks sprayed from its jaws.

Warriors swarmed to meet it, staffs glowing as they struck. The clash rattled the cavern, roots groaning against the impact. Selena spun into the fray, her purple whirlwind flashing like a phantom storm. Kimilo darted low, staff crackling as she struck at the beast's legs.

Perrin slammed her palms against the barrier. "Let me out! I can help!"

No one answered. Her voice drowned in the roar of battle, in the guttural bellow of the Belofez as it swung its head, scattering fighters like dolls.

Her throat burned. She gripped the staff tight, willing it to unlock the barrier, to let her join them. It pulsed once, steady but unmoving.

She could do nothing. Nothing but watch as the village bled and fought while she stood locked away, useless.

A child's scream pierced the chaos, cut off by an elder pulling them to safety. Perrin's chest collapsed in on itself. This wasn't punishment anymore. It was torture.

She pressed her forehead against the roots, tears stinging hot. "Please," she whispered to the staff. "Don't make me just watch."

The staff thrummed, low and cryptic, but the roots held firm.

The battle outside rolled on, each crash of the Belofez rattling Perrin's bones. She clung to the barrier, fists white, eyes burning as Selena's whirlwind split the air and Kimilo's staff sparked against scale. They were brilliant, unstoppable—and still the beast raged.

Then, through the thunder, her staff began to hum. Not faint, not subtle this time, but sharp and clear. She jerked back, clutching it tight against her chest.

The hum folded into words.

They cannot end him. Not this one.

Perrin's breath caught. "Then who can?"

You.

The single word struck harder than any Contrary sphere. Her knees buckled, and she sat back hard on the stone. "Me? I can't even keep from hurting Garantuke. I can't even keep my own jealousy from wrecking everything. Why would I be the one?"

The staff's glow spread across her lap, pulsing like a heartbeat.

Because the shadow waits for you. Because blood

remembers the generations before you. Because only you can face him.

Her stomach twisted. Only her. No Selena. No Kimilo. Not even Garantuke. Just her.

She shook her head, hot tears sliding down her cheeks. "I'm fourteen. I'm not— I'm not some warrior. I don't even know what I'm doing."

The staff flared brighter, searing her palms. Not cruel, not burning, but insistent.

Not yet. But you will.

The words sank into her chest, settling heavy beside her fear. She wanted to throw the staff away, to deny it— but her fingers wouldn't let go.

Outside, the Belofez roared, and the cavern shook again. Inside, Perrin's pulse echoed the staff's light, refusing to let her hide.

The echoes of the staff's words still thrummed in Perrin's ears when a different sound caught her attention —a soft scrape outside her cell, slower and more hesitant than the warriors rushing past.

She pressed to the roots, peering through the narrow slit.

A figure stood in the shadows beyond the torch-fungus glow. One of the Contrary Men—she recognized the backward-tipped hat, the beige vest. But he wasn't like the others. His movements weren't jerky or mocking. He stood still, his head tilted toward her cell as though listening.

Perrin's skin prickled.

He didn't speak, not in the twisted, backward babble she'd heard before. Instead, his hand lifted halfway, trembling, then lowered again.

For a moment their eyes met through the glow. His gaze wasn't hollow like the others. Something stirred there—confusion, maybe pain, but also... recognition.

Her breath caught.

The staff hummed faintly in her hands, but not in warning. It felt almost... softer. Curious.

The man shifted, stepping closer. His lips parted, and a broken whisper scraped out, warped but still almost words. "Fre end."

Friend?

Perrin's throat tightened. The sound struck too deep, too familiar.

Before she could respond, shouts rang from the far end of the corridor. The man stiffened, eyes wide, then backed into the shadows until he vanished.

Perrin stayed at the slit long after he was gone, her chest hollow, her staff pulsing gently against her palms.

Who was he—and why did that one word feel like it had torn open something buried inside her?

The next day, voices stirred outside her cell again. This time, she didn't rush to the slit. She braced herself first, afraid of what she might—or might not—see.

When she finally looked, Garantuke stood there.

He wasn't alone—two elders flanked him, their gazes

stern, watching to ensure he obeyed the ban. But his eyes found hers instantly, even through the narrow weave of roots.

For a long moment, neither spoke. His jaw worked, as though he wanted to say something but couldn't with the elders there. His hand twitched at his side, half a reach toward her, then curled into a fist.

Perrin's breath hitched. The look on his face—it wasn't just disappointment. It wasn't just anger. It was heavier, layered, like grief and longing tangled together.

She pressed her fingers through the roots, aching to touch him, to explain, to apologize. "I didn't mean—"

The elder barked a sharp word, and Garantuke flinched. His gaze softened with something perilously close to sorrow. Then he looked away, turning his back to her.

The roots blurred as Perrin's eyes stung. *He hates me,* her mind insisted. But the ache in his eyes told a different story. He cared. He just couldn't show it—not here, not now.

That made it worse.

She slid down the wall, clutching her staff close. Her chest ached with the weight of his silence, his sorrow. If he had screamed at her, she could have borne it. But that look... that look would haunt her.

Night fell heavy, the chamber colder than before. Perrin lay awake, staff clutched to her chest. Every sound from the village—the distant ring of hammers, the low murmur of voices—felt like a reminder of the life carrying on without her.

Her thoughts circled endlessly: the elders' anger, the devastation of the Belofez, the shadowed man whispering *friend*, and, worst of all, the weight in Garantuke's eyes. Love and disappointment twined together, breaking her open in ways no punishment could.

The staff pulsed faintly, steady as a heartbeat. She closed her eyes and listened.

This time, there were no riddles. No cryptic fragments. Just a sense of quiet expectation, like Miketo itself was waiting.

Perrin breathed deep, tasting the damp earth, the faint tang of root-sap. She pressed her palms tighter around the staff until the ridges bit into her skin.

"I'm done messing up," she whispered. "Done letting anger, or jealousy, or anything else decide for me. If you chose me, then fine. But I'll listen this time. I'll respect you. I'll learn."

The staff flared, light spilling across the chamber in a single sharp pulse. Then it settled, warm against her hands.

Perrin leaned back, eyes burning but dry. For the first time since she'd fallen into this place, she felt something stir that wasn't guilt or fear.

Resolve.

"I'll be ready," she murmured into the silence. "I have to

be."

Outside, the cavern quieted. But within her chest, the vow burned bright.

CHAPTER 11: READINESS

The Hall of Scrolls pulsed with root-light, every carved glyph alive with a faint shimmer. Perrin stood in the center, her staff gripped so tight her palms ached. The air pressed heavy around her, filled with the elders' silence.

She had been summoned without explanation. Guards flanked the doors, and the villagers gathered in the shadows, watching. Judging.

Then, without her moving a finger, the staff flared. Blue light surged up its length, brighter than a torch, spilling across the stone floor.

The elders stiffened.

A voice—not spoken, not hers—filled the hall. It resonated from the staff itself, carried through every ear and bone.

She is ready.

Gasps broke out. Perrin's heart stopped.

The eldest elder leaned forward, his gnarled hands trembling on his staff. "Miketo speaks."

Another hissed, incredulous. "It cannot mean *her*. Not

after the chaos she's caused."

The staff pulsed again, silencing them.

She alone may walk the path.

The words rang final, leaving no room for debate. Even the roots in the walls glowed brighter, as though in agreement.

Perrin swallowed hard, heat crawling up her throat. She hadn't asked for this. She hadn't earned it—or had she? Her vow in the cell came back to her, sharp and clear. *I'll listen this time. I'll respect you.*

Now Miketo itself was calling her bluff.

The elders exchanged uneasy glances. None dared challenge the voice again.

Perrin tightened her grip, the weight of destiny suddenly heavier than the staff in her hands.

The crowd dispersed slowly, whispers chasing Perrin like gnats, but three figures stepped forward through the hush.

Selena came first, her dark hair falling like a curtain over her shoulder. Her eyes glimmered with something unspoken, and for the first time Perrin thought she saw relief there. Selena pressed her hand lightly to Perrin's staff. A faint shimmer of violet flickered between them.

"Walk steady," Selena murmured. "You carry more than yourself now." Her tone was gentle, but beneath it Perrin heard the truth: Selena had carried that same weight once, maybe still did.

Kimilo followed, her movements crisp and deliberate.

She bowed formally, then lifted Perrin's hand and set it against her own heart. "Do not fight like me," she said in her clipped, accented voice. "Fight like *you*. That is the only way Miketo will honor you."

Perrin blinked. She had expected criticism, sharp edges. Instead, Kimilo offered something deeper— permission to be herself, not a shadow of someone else's training.

Then the air shifted, and Moonshadow was simply *there*. No footsteps, no warning, just light blue skin gleaming faintly in the root-light. Her gaze settled on Perrin, ancient and piercing, as if she could see every mistake, every doubt still knotted inside her.

"Eric is Malum," she said again, but this time it wasn't a warning. It was a charge. A reminder of what lay ahead.

Moonshadow lifted her palm, brushing a fingertip just over Perrin's brow without touching. A rush of cool air swept through her mind, carrying an echo of words not entirely her own.

Blood remembers your ancestors. Do not forget who you are.

Perrin's breath caught. When she looked again, Moonshadow had already dissolved into the dim edges of the hall, leaving only the faint echo of her presence.

Perrin stood there, the blessings of three different women woven into her like threads, each one both comforting and terrifying.

After the blessings, Perrin expected—no, *needed*—to

see him. Garantuke.

She left the Hall, clutching her staff as villagers parted for her. Some looked at her with awe, others with suspicion, but she barely noticed. Her gaze swept the crowd again and again, hunting for his broad shoulders, his steady eyes.

Nothing.

She crossed the training grounds, her boots crunching against stone. He wasn't sparring there. She peered toward the root bridges, hoping to find him directing repairs. Empty. Even the Healing Halls, where she knew his ribs still ached, held no sign of him.

Her chest tightened. Of course he wasn't here. The elders had probably warned him away, just as they had before. But part of her had hoped he would defy them this time. That he would be waiting in some shadowed corner, ready to tell her she wasn't alone.

The staff pulsed faintly in her grip, as though reminding her she wasn't abandoned, not entirely. But it wasn't the same.

Perrin slowed at the edge of the cavern, staring out into the dark where the Allekanu Path began. Her heart tugged backward, toward him, even as destiny pulled her forward.

"He doesn't even care enough to say goodbye," she whispered, though the sting in her eyes betrayed the lie. She knew he cared. That was the problem.

But if he wouldn't stand by her now, she would stand

on her own.

She squared her shoulders, clutching the staff tight. Determination wrapped around her grief like armor. If she had to face Malum alone, then so be it.

The Allekanu Path yawned before her, its spiraling glyphs faintly glowing along the stone walls. The air that seeped from it was colder than the village behind her, laced with whispers that crawled along her skin.

A small group of villagers had gathered to watch her go. Selena and Kimilo stood together, their eyes steady, blessings already given. Elders lingered farther back, silent, their verdict carried in the staff's earlier declaration. Perrin searched their faces one last time for some sign of approval—or even hope—but found none.

Her gaze swept over the crowd once more, straining for the figure she knew wouldn't be there. No broad shoulders. No steady eyes. Garantuke had kept his distance.

Her chest squeezed. She wanted to scream, to beg him to appear. But instead, she drew a deep breath and forced her chin high.

"This time," she whispered to herself, fingers tightening on the staff, "I won't let emotion wreck me. Not anger. Not jealousy. Not heartbreak. I'll finish this."

The staff pulsed, its glow meeting the glyph-light of the Path, as if affirming her vow.

Perrin stepped forward, each footfall a quiet rebellion against her fear. With every step, the village receded into silence until she stood alone at the mouth of the Path.

She looked back only once. The people of Tuspin were shadows against the glow, unmoving, waiting. Waiting to see if she would succeed—or if she would be just another reckless mistake.

Heart splintered, spirit taut, Perrin turned away. Determination carried her into the darkness.

The Allekanu Path swallowed her whole. Its walls twisted upward, spirals of ancient glyphs etched deep into the stone, glowing faintly like veins of trapped lightning. Every mark seemed alive, shifting just out of focus, whispering promises or threats she couldn't quite hear.

Last time she had walked here, fear had ruled her. Every shadow had seemed ready to lunge, every whisper had sunk claws into her nerves. She had lashed out without thought, her Miketo rebounding against her and leaving her broken.

But now... now her grip on the staff was steady. Her breathing matched the faint rhythm of its pulses. Fear still licked at the edges of her thoughts, but it didn't own her anymore.

The first defenses appeared—floating orbs of light drifting from the walls, humming with the same resonance as before when the Contrary Men hurled them at her. Perrin's heart jolted, memory screaming *run*. Instead, she stilled her racing thoughts, focusing on the hum. It wasn't random. It had a pattern. A rhythm.

She matched her own pulse to it, raising her staff slowly. The orbs wavered. Instead of attacking blindly, she nudged them, guiding their energy aside. They floated back, dissolving into the stone as if acknowledging her restraint.

A smile flickered across her lips—small, but real.

Step by step, she pressed forward, each trial on the Path testing her. The psychic whispers grew sharper, hissing doubts: *You are reckless. You will fail. He will crush you.* Perrin's chest tightened, but she gritted her teeth, whispering back, "Not this time."

Every successful step forward wasn't just progress down the Path—it was proof that she wasn't the same girl who had stormed out in anger.

The darkness ahead loomed thicker, but for the first time, Perrin felt stronger walking into it.

The Path narrowed into a jagged throat of stone. Perrin slowed, staff raised, senses bristling. She wasn't alone.

Two figures emerged from the shadows ahead, their movements stiff and unnatural. Guards. Not an army, not the swarming tide she had once imagined, but two Contrary Men standing firm across the passage. Their top hats tilted backward, beige coats buttoned tight, faces slack and eyes unfocused.

Her stomach clenched. The memory of their mocking backward speech and painful energy spheres licked at her nerves. But this time, she didn't rush. She studied them.

Both stepped in unison, backward strides echoing

strangely. One lifted a hand, conjuring a sphere of glowing energy. It pulsed erratically, like a heartbeat off rhythm.

Perrin's grip tightened on her staff. She centered her breathing, recalling Kimilo's sharp precision and Selena's calm control.

The first sphere launched. She angled her staff, not striking hard but guiding the energy just as she had with the Path's orbs. The sphere hissed past her, slamming harmlessly into the wall.

The guards staggered, confusion flashing across their faces. Perrin seized the moment, darting forward. She tapped her staff against the second guard's conjured sphere, letting Miketo's hum override its unstable core. It fizzled out in a crackle of light, leaving the guard momentarily stunned.

Perrin's heart pounded. Not fear—exhilaration. She could do this.

She swept her staff low, striking at the roots beneath their feet. The ground shifted, living vines snapping up to bind their boots. The guards struggled, jerky motions slowing as the roots held fast.

For the first time, she wasn't humiliated, wasn't broken by her own impatience. She had taken control.

She exhaled, steady, watching the glow fade from their conjured spheres. "Tell Eric I'm not afraid anymore," she muttered, though she knew they couldn't hear her through the fog in their minds.

And then she stepped past them, deeper into the fortress's shadow.

The Path widened into a cavern where the air vibrated faintly, carrying voices ahead. Perrin slowed, crouching behind a jagged outcrop of stone. The torch fungi here burned dimmer, leaving patches of darkness that cloaked her.

Eric's voice drifted through the air, smooth and commanding, though sharper now than the practiced charm he had used at school.

"They will not turn against me," he said, his words echoing faintly. "They fear me too much for that."

Perrin crept closer, heart thudding, until she caught sight of him through a narrow break in the rock. Eric stood with half a dozen followers arrayed around him, their eyes lowered, their bodies rigid. No admiration glowed there, no loyalty—only tension, like animals trained under the whip.

One follower dared to speak, his voice trembling. "But if they outnumber us—if Nimrodabbi's group refuses—"

Eric cut him off with a sharp gesture, his smile thin as a blade. "Fear holds them tighter than chains. Love wavers. Loyalty can be broken. But fear... fear is eternal."

The words hit Perrin like a strike. So that was his strength—not devotion, not unity, but the same thing he had done to her at school. Manipulate. Compel. Bend until people snapped under his control.

Her grip tightened on her staff until her knuckles

ached. She thought of Garantuke's eyes filled with sorrow, of Selena and Kimilo standing shoulder to shoulder, of Moonshadow's warning. That was what true strength looked like—not fear, but connection.

And Eric had none of it.

She leaned back into the shadow, steadying her breath. For the first time, she didn't just feel afraid of him. She saw his weakness.

Perrin eased away from the outcrop, careful not to disturb a stone. She turned deeper into the shadows, following the staff's faint hum guiding her around a side corridor. The air grew colder, heavy with a metallic tang.

Then she felt it—a prickle at the back of her neck. She wasn't alone.

She spun, staff raised, ready to strike.

A figure stepped from the dark. One of the Contrary Men. Beige vest buttoned, top hat tilted back, movements slow and uneven. But his eyes... they weren't hollow like the others. They caught hers, flickering with recognition that made her chest seize.

The staff pulsed once, softer than a warning, almost like acknowledgment.

Perrin froze, torn between fear and the strange pull in her gut.

The man lifted a trembling hand, pointing toward the wall ahead. His voice came broken, backward-twisted, but she could still catch fragments. "Tr...ap. Not...that way."

Her breath caught. He wasn't attacking. He was warning her.

He stepped closer, pulling something from beneath his coat—a stone set in a crude iron clasp, its glow faint but steady. The Star-Stone. Garantuke said it was beautiful, but this was far beyond that simple description.

Her mouth went dry. That was what Garantuke's father had died protecting. What Eric had stolen.

The Contrary Man's hand shook as he held it out to her. For a heartbeat, she couldn't move. Then, with a trembling reach, she took it.

The stone's glow surged the instant it touched her skin, light running like liquid down the length of her staff.

The man's gaze softened. He whispered one more broken word, voice raw and cracked. "Fr...end."

Her throat closed.

Before she could answer, shouts rang out from deeper in the fortress. The man flinched, retreating into shadow, vanishing as quickly as he'd come.

Perrin clutched the Star-Stone against her chest, her heart racing. Whoever he was, whatever part of him still fought against Malum's grip—he had chosen to help her.

And now she carried both the staff and the Star-Stone.

Destiny had no more excuses left for her.

The glow of the Star-Stone throbbed against her palm, its light flowing into the staff until both pulsed as one. Perrin stood in the narrow corridor, chest heaving, the weight of everything pressing in—Garantuke's absence, the elders' doubts, Moonshadow's warning, the whispers of the staff, even the broken word from the Contrary Man who felt too much like family to be coincidence.

The fortress loomed ahead, its walls glimmering with oily reflections, alive and waiting. Shadows curled along the archway, like Eric himself had shaped them to watch her.

Fear rose sharp and bitter, the same fear that had driven her into mistake after mistake. She let it wash through her, not fighting, just feeling it. Then she tightened her grip on the staff, the Star-Stone warm against her skin, and breathed it out.

Not fear. Not jealousy. Not anger. Not anymore.

Her voice came steady, firmer than she expected, carrying down the corridor into the dark. "I am ready."

The words rang truer than anything she had spoken since falling into this world.

The staff pulsed once, strong and sure, as if Miketo itself agreed.

And Perrin stepped forward toward the heart of Malum's hold.

CHAPTER 12: THE ARENA

The Star-Stone was heavy in her hand, so Perrin looked it over saw a way to attached it to her belt before she continued forward. The corridor widened abruptly, and Perrin stepped out into a cavern that dwarfed anything she had seen in Tuspin. The ceiling soared high above, lost in shadow, while the floor stretched into a vast ring of polished obsidian. Glyphs burned along its edges, pulsing with a sickly red glow that made the whole place feel alive, like she had walked straight into the belly of a beast.

And waiting at its heart was Eric.

He stood tall, a flawless figure in dark clothes that shimmered faintly, his smile sharp as glass. His eyes locked onto hers the moment she entered, gleaming with the same unnerving confidence he had worn the first day she saw him at school.

Around him, followers packed the stone benches carved into the cavern walls. Dozens of them—Contrary Men and villagers alike—sat in stiff silence, their eyes unfocused, their hands clenched on their knees. No cheers, no whispers, just the hollow presence of people bent under his control.

Her chest tightened. He had made them into an audience for her failure.

Eric spread his arms wide, as if presenting her to them. "At last," he said, voice echoing across the chamber. "The little girl who thought she could defy me."

Perrin's staff pulsed, its glow steady, but she felt every eye on her. Her throat went dry, but she forced herself forward, each step landing with a sharp strike against the obsidian floor.

If this was his stage, then she would play her part.

Perrin lifted her staff, drawing strength from its hum. The blue glow rippled along its length, spilling light over the obsidian floor. For a moment, she felt steadied— anchored by Miketo's presence.

Eric's smile deepened. He raised his hand lazily, as though brushing away a cobweb.

The light on her staff flickered.

Perrin's pulse stuttered. She tightened her grip, willing the glow back. "Stay with me," she whispered.

But the hum sputtered into nothing, like a candle snuffed by a sudden wind. The blue faded to black. The staff sagged in her hands, heavy now, as if its heart had been torn out.

Gasps rippled through the benches. Not from awe, but from the shifting, uneasy silence of those who'd seen their one hope gutter out.

Eric laughed. The sound was low, rich, and cruel. "Did you think Miketo would protect you here? This is my arena. My will commands the stones, the air, even the staff you cling to like a child's toy."

Perrin's throat tightened. She lifted the staff again, though it felt lifeless, and forced her voice to remain steady. "You can't silence me."

Eric tilted his head, amused. "I already have."

The emptiness where the staff's hum had been pressed down on her like a weight. For a heartbeat, panic clawed at her chest. But beneath it, something else stirred—anger, sharp and hot.

Not at Miketo. Not at the staff. At *him*.

Eric began to circle her, his boots clicking against the obsidian floor, each step echoing too loud in the cavern. His followers' eyes tracked him, not her, as though they were strings pulled by his movement.

"You never saw it, did you?" he said, voice dripping with satisfaction. "From the very first moment. The stumble on the school stairs? That wasn't clumsiness. That was me."

Perrin's chest tightened. Her knees remembered the sting of that fall, the heat of humiliation when she'd tripped in front of everyone.

"I wanted you to feel small," Eric went on, circling closer. "And you did. Every gasp, every laugh from your classmates was mine. I whispered doubt into you, and you carried it like a badge."

Her grip on the useless staff whitened.

"And when I told you to take those keys," he added, lips curling in mock pity, "you didn't hesitate. You *wanted* to please me, Perrin. You wanted to be wanted, even if it meant betraying your friends. Don't deny it."

Heat burned her cheeks. Her lungs filled too fast, too shallow.

Eric leaned close, his words meant only for her now. "You're here because I made you. Every step you've taken has been mine. You are nothing without me."

The arena seemed to press in, the whispers of the enthralled crowd echoing in her skull. For a heartbeat, she teetered on the edge of believing him.

Then her staff pulsed once—not with light, but with the faintest vibration against her palm. Enough to remind her of her vow.

Her jaw clenched. Maybe he had tripped her. Maybe he had whispered lies. But every mistake after had been hers —and she had survived them.

Her vision blurred with heat. She wanted to scream, to swing the staff at Eric's smug face until the obsidian cracked beneath him. Every taunt fanned the fire that had always lived inside her—the same fire that had driven her to storm out, to lash first and think later, to keep proving him right.

Her knuckles whitened on the dead weight of the staff. "You think you control me?" she snapped, voice raw. "You think every mistake I made was because of *you*? Maybe you tripped me. Maybe you whispered. But you didn't make me jealous. You didn't make me impatient. Those were mine. And I survived them anyway."

Eric's smile faltered, just a fraction.

The crowd shifted. A murmur ran through them, like a ripple across stillwater.

Perrin inhaled slowly, forcing the fire down, pressing it into something sharper. Not rage—clarity. Her pulse steadied. Her breath came even. For the first time in this place, she wasn't reacting to him. She was choosing her own response.

She lifted the lifeless staff, holding it steady like a blade. "You didn't break me. You only showed me what I had to fix."

Eric's eyes narrowed, the easy arrogance slipping at the edges.

And in that sliver of hesitation, Perrin saw it—the weakness he had just admitted himself: fear was all he had. And fear worked only if she gave it room.

Perrin straightened, her voice carrying further now, no longer just for him but for everyone forced to watch.

"You bragged to your followers," she said, each word deliberate, "that fear keeps them loyal. That they'll never turn on you because they're too afraid."

Eric stiffened, the faintest twitch in his jaw.

Perrin pressed on, louder, letting her words strike where his pride lived. "But fear doesn't last. Fear fades. It rots. And the second they see you slip, the second they see you lose..." She let her gaze sweep deliberately over the rows of blank-eyed followers. "...they'll remember what it feels like to hate you."

Eric's smile cracked. "They don't hate me," he spat, the smooth calm gone from his voice. "They *need* me."

Perrin tilted her head, feigning thought. "No... I think they're just waiting. Waiting for someone to show them you're not as strong as you pretend."

A restless stir spread through the benches, a subtle sound of shuffling boots and uneasy breaths. Perrin felt it—their attention tilting toward her, even through the haze of Eric's control.

Eric's composure frayed. He lunged a step closer, jabbing a finger at her. "You think a child can undo me? You? You're nothing but a mistake with a stick."

Her staff remained lifeless, but her voice rang clear. "Funny. That mistake is standing here while you're screaming in your own arena."

A growl tore from his throat, his veneer finally gone.

And Perrin knew she had him.

Eric moved first. He slashed his hand through the air, and the obsidian floor rippled like water. Spikes of stone erupted in a jagged line toward her.

Perrin dodged left, heart hammering, but she didn't lash out. She kept her breathing steady, recalling Kimilo's sharp discipline, Selena's calm rhythm.

Eric's voice boomed as he hurled another wave of power. "Kneel, Perrin! You were mine from the start—you will end on your knees!"

The words cut deep, dragging up the memory of the school stairwell, the laughter, the shame. Her pulse stuttered, panic clawing up her throat.

She gritted her teeth. *That was then. That's not me now.*

She steadied her stance, planting the staff like an anchor, even though it remained dark. Instead of rushing, she waited—watching.

Eric stormed closer, fury twisting his perfect features. He lashed out again, sending a sphere of crackling energy toward her. She didn't block it head-on. She shifted, angled, let it pass. The blast exploded against the far wall, harmless.

Gasps rippled through the benches.

Perrin's lips curved into a thin smile. "You miss when I don't play your game."

Eric snarled, his control fraying further. He attacked again and again, each strike faster, sloppier. She moved with patience, sidestepping, guiding blasts away, letting his own rage eat him alive.

The murmurs in the audience grew louder, no longer just shuffling but whispers—fear unraveling into doubt.

For every mistake Eric made, Perrin grew steadier. She didn't need the staff's hum. She had her clarity, and it was enough.

At last, he stumbled, his own blast rebounding off a twisted spike and knocking him to his knees.

The arena went silent.

Perrin stood tall, staff firm in her grip, breath steady. For once, she wasn't the one collapsing.

Eric struggled on his knees, his hands braced against the floor as if the obsidian itself were slipping away beneath him. The polished sheen of his perfect image was gone—sweat streaked his brow, his breath came ragged, and his eyes darted with something Perrin had never seen in him before. Fear.

The crowd stirred. For the first time, their gazes shifted not with his gestures, but with their own awareness, their own choices.

One voice broke the silence, hoarse and trembling: "He's... weak."

Another followed, louder: "He lied to us."

Eric whipped his head toward them, desperation cracking his tone. "No! You obey me! You *fear* me!" He thrust out his hand, trying to tighten invisible strings— but nothing happened. His powers puttered, like a flame choking on its own smoke.

The followers rose from their benches, slow at first, then faster, a tide of movement. Some shouted. Some hurled curses. Others simply turned away, shaking free of the haze that had held them.

Eric reached for them with his voice, his last weapon, but every word now sounded hollow, broken by the proof before their eyes.

Perrin stepped closer, her staff steady, her voice cutting across the arena. "Fear doesn't last, Eric. Not when people see the truth."

A roar went up—not for him, but against him. Followers stormed the steps down into the arena. Some threw stones, others spat at his feet. A handful seized him by the arms, jerking him upright only to shove him forward.

Eric stumbled, collapsing at Perrin's feet. His earlier arrogance was gone, his smile shattered. All that remained was a boy who had mistaken control for strength—and lost both.

Eric's chest heaved as he knelt before her, sweat and fury dripping together. The oily sheen of the arena's light no longer made him untouchable—it only highlighted how small he suddenly looked.

At her belt, secured in a clasp of black iron, the Star-Stone glimmered faintly.

Perrin lowered her staff, her voice steady. "This never belonged to you."

Eric snarled. "Give that back! It's mine! I took it, I bled for it—power answers to me!"

The Star-Stone pulsed sharply, rejecting him, and a cry of pain ripped from his throat.

Perrin stepped closer. She simply extended her hand, palm open, calm. "No, Eric. Power answers to respect. And it knows you'll never have that."

For a breathless moment, nothing happened. Then, with a shudder like glass cracking, the iron clasp split apart and the Star-Stone wrenched free and shot into

Perrin's waiting hand, glowing brighter the instant it touched her skin.

The arena erupted in gasps and cries. The glow ran down her arm into the staff, and for the first time since entering the arena, its hum roared back to life—steady, strong, undeniable.

Eric collapsed forward, clutching his empty hands, a broken sound tearing from his throat.

Perrin stood over him, Star-Stone in one hand, staff blazing in the other. She felt no triumph, only the certainty that the fight was over.

The hum of the staff filled the arena, rolling like thunder against the obsidian walls. Perrin stood tall, light streaming from the Star-Stone through her hands, no longer just a girl with reckless impulses but a figure every pair of eyes in that chamber was forced to see.

Eric crumpled at her feet, his shoulders shaking. The defiance in his eyes was gone, drowned beneath exhaustion and the unraveling of the lies he had woven around himself. His followers no longer looked at him with fear—they looked with contempt, some with disgust, and a few with pity.

"You made me think I was nothing," Perrin said quietly, her voice carrying in the silence. "But you're the one who was hollow. Everything you had came from stealing—stealing fear, stealing trust, stealing power that was never yours."

Eric raised his head, lips trembling around words that

never came.

Perrin's staff blazed once more, the glow flaring across the chamber like sunrise breaking a long night. The benches shook with the sound of his followers turning away from him, their chains broken. Several of his former followers lifted Malum up and clasped chains around him to keep his hands and feet immovable.

The boy who had once seemed invincible now stood shattered, surrounded by those he had ruled. A woman strode forward and bowed with respect to Perrin. "Please miss, take him away to pay for his crimes. We'll send someone to get the keys that will open the place where he keeps treasures. Take them as well to return to those he stole them from."

Perrin drew a long, steady breath. The fight was finished. But her journey wasn't. "Yes, that is the right thing to do."

She turned from her, the Star-Stone pulsing in her palm, and looked toward the fortress doors that loomed beyond. Shadows curled there, waiting. A path forward. A path home.

The staff whispered in her hand, not words but a certainty.

This was only the beginning.

CHAPTER 13: THE RETURN TO TUSPIN

The fortress walls seemed smaller now, less a place of terror than a husk already collapsing without its master's will to bind it. Perrin stood at the threshold, staff in one hand and the Star-Stone glowing in the other, and for the first time since falling into this world she felt the weight of choice pressing harder than fear.

She could stay. She could train, grow, maybe even belong among those who had finally stopped looking at her as an intruder.

But the image of her mother's face rose sharp in her mind—the worry lines deepened, the harsh voice softened by guilt she'd only just begun to understand. The thought of Pandra waiting above, not knowing whether her daughter was alive or gone forever, cinched the decision before doubt could creep in.

Her chest tightened, equal parts dread and determination. It wasn't enough to have defeated Eric. She had to put right the things he'd twisted—her own mistakes included.

Perrin adjusted her grip on the staff, the stone's light flowing down its length like it already knew where she was going. "I'm going home," she whispered, more to herself than anyone else.

And for once, the words didn't sound like a child's wish. They sounded like a promise.

When Perrin stepped back into the outer halls, the crowd that had once sat entranced under Eric's control now moved with restless energy. Freed from his voice, they looked dazed, some ashamed, others furious. Yet when she passed, their eyes shifted with something new —respect. Some of the Contrary Men that had mocked and attacked her mouthed apologies the best they could. "I forgive you," was her reply.

One of the villagers, a heavyset man in a tattered vest, stepped forward, avoiding her gaze at first. In his hands, he held a ring of iron keys. "He... kept what he stole here," he said, voice low, as though confessing a sin.

Others beckoned her down a side corridor. Perrin followed, her staff lighting the way until they reached a chamber lined with crude iron cages. Inside lay a jumble of possessions: crates of tools, jewelry, books, trinkets —things taken from both Tuspin and travelers unlucky enough to stumble near the fortress. Even things from the above world.

And there, shoved between broken furniture and boxes, sat the teacher's car. Its frame was scratched, its windows dusty, but otherwise whole, gleaming faintly as though it remembered the sunlight it had been denied.

Perrin's breath caught. That car had been the start of everything—the theft, the blame, the suspension, her fall into this world. Seeing it here, trapped and out of place, was like looking at a piece of her old life locked in a cage.

The man with the iron keys pressed them into her palm. "The treasures are yours to do with as you wish," he said, not quite meeting her eyes. Around them, other freed followers murmured, some apologizing, others spitting curses at Eric's name.

Perrin curled her fingers around the keys. This wasn't just about proving herself to them. It was about setting things right above, where it had all begun.

Perrin walked a slow circle around the car, her staff's glow washing over the metal. The machine looked almost ridiculous here in the underworld, surrounded by cages and roots and shadows. Yet it pulled at her like a magnet —a reminder of her mistakes, of how easily she had been swayed by Eric's voice, and how quickly everyone had believed the worst of her.

Her fingers traced the hood, leaving streaks in the dust. In her reflection she saw not the scared girl who had grabbed those keys at school, but someone different— someone who had fought, bled, and chosen her own path.

"I'm bringing this back," she said firmly. Her voice carried through the chamber, startling even herself with its certainty. "Not just the car—everything he took. All of it's going back where it belongs, one way or another."

Some of Eric's ex-followers exchanged glances, then nodded. Others bowed their heads in quiet agreement. Two excitedly explained what treasures came from where. Apparently, Tuspin was not the only village below ground. "If you know who the true owners are, see that they get back what was taken from them."

Perrin found the car keys sitting on the front seat. She was going to reach for them, but the button for the trunk caught her eye on the dashboard. She pressed the button and the trunk opened. "Put Malum in there, please."

Eric did not even protest as his ex-followers lifted him and dropped him in the trunk of the concept car. They shut the trunk and added some rude goodbyes to him before stepping away.

Perrin clenched the ring of keys in her fist. This wasn't just about clearing her name anymore. It was about making sure no one could say Eric had the last word, or that Perrin Roberts was still the impulsive girl who couldn't think ahead.

Her gaze lifted to the fortress doors, already imagining sunlight streaming over them. "I'll make it right," she whispered. "Every last piece."

As Perrin lingered by the car, the murmurs of the freed followers faded into the background. She didn't notice when someone stepped up beside her until a familiar shadow crossed the dusty hood.

Garantuke.

He looked tired—his tunic torn from a battle she

wasn't aware of, dark hair plastered to his forehead—but his eyes were steady, fixed on her with a weight that made her throat tighten.

"You've done what none of us could," he said quietly, almost reverently. "Malum is broken. The paths he closed off centuries ago are free again."

Perrin swallowed. She wanted to bask in the praise, but there was something in his tone that sounded like a farewell.

"I have to go back," she said quickly, before he could say it. "My mom doesn't know if I'm alive. I need to clear my name at school. I need to... finish what started there."

Garantuke studied her for a long moment, the silence stretching heavy between them. She braced for his refusal —for him to remind her of his duty, of Tuspin, of everything he couldn't abandon.

Instead, he exhaled slowly and nodded. "Then I'll go with you."

Her heart skipped. "What? But... Tuspin—your people need you."

"They have Selena. They have Kimilo. They even have Moonshadow when she chooses." His jaw tightened. "But you..." He paused, searching for words. "You've become more than a stranger who stumbled into our world. You've become my choice. And I won't let you face yours alone."

Perrin blinked fast, her throat tightening. For a moment, she couldn't think of anything clever to say. All she managed was a soft, shaky: "You really mean that?"

"I do." His voice was firm, leaving no space for doubt.

The chamber brightened suddenly, not with Perrin's staff or the Star-Stone, but with a soft silver glow that seemed to bleed in from nowhere. The freed followers gasped and stepped back as Moonshadow appeared in their midst, her light-blue skin shimmering faintly beneath the glow.

Her smoke-gray eyes fixed first on Perrin, then on Garantuke. "So," she said, her voice calm but carrying through the chamber like a bell, "the choice is made."

Perrin straightened, still clutching the car keys. "He said he's coming with me. But I don't want Tuspin left unprotected."

Moonshadow tilted her head. "Tuspin is not so fragile as you think. Selena has the strength of a Flame, Kimilo the discipline of one taught with love. The elders will guide the village, and Miketo itself watches over those who respect it."

She turned her gaze on Garantuke, her expression unreadable. "But if you leave, you leave as more than a warrior. You leave as one who must carry both love and loss."

Garantuke didn't flinch. "I know my duty. And my choice."

For a long, tense heartbeat, Moonshadow seemed to weigh his words. Then she inclined her head, a faint smile ghosting across her lips. "Then it is permitted. Tuspin will endure, and your path will be beside her."

The glow around her softened, dimming until only her eyes still held the glimmer of distant fire. "Do not mistake this as an end. Choices always carry consequences—yours no less than hers."

With that, she faded into silver motes, leaving the chamber hushed and awed.

Perrin exhaled, her heart racing. For the first time, no barrier stood between her and home.

The silence Moonshadow left behind pressed on Perrin until she couldn't hold it anymore. She turned sharply to Garantuke, words tumbling out before fear could stop them.

"There's something I need to know. That girl you hugged." Her voice cracked slightly as she said it. "Back in the village... when I saw you with her, when you hugged her—I thought..." She bit her lip, heat rising in her face. "I thought maybe that's why you didn't want to come with me. That she was the reason you'd stay."

Garantuke blinked, then exhaled, shaking his head with a mix of amusement and exasperation. "Perrin." His voice softened, though the steel in it remained. "Luda is my cousin. My mother's sister's daughter. She was helping me plan a gift for you—one I wasn't ready to give then. That hug was gratitude, not... anything else."

Perrin's stomach dropped. Her heart, tight with weeks of jealousy and fear, untwisted in a single painful rush. "So I... I made all that up in my head."

His mouth curved in the faintest smile. "You made it up because you care. That much, at least, I understand."

She groaned, burying her face in her hands. "I was such an idiot. I almost ruined everything."

"You didn't ruin it," he said simply. "You only made the path harder to walk. But that path led here."

Perrin lowered her hands, meeting his steady gaze. The shame was still there, but now it carried a strange kind of relief. The shadow of Luda was gone, and in its place, something clearer settled between them.

For once, she didn't need to argue. She just nodded.

The Star-Stone throbbed in Perrin's palm, warm and alive, its glow steady now that Eric's grip was broken. She stared down at it, remembering how desperately Eric had wanted it back, how it had chosen her when he claimed it was his.

She turned to Garantuke, her throat tight. "This doesn't belong to me. It belongs to Tuspin. To you."

He stiffened, eyes widening. "Perrin, no—"

But she pressed it into his hands before he could refuse. The glow swelled, spilling between his fingers until it lit his face in blue-gold. His jaw trembled, and for the first time since she'd met him, she saw him falter— not from battle, not from anger, but from raw, unguarded feeling.

"It was my father's charge," he whispered, voice breaking. "He died trying to protect it. I thought I'd never be worthy to hold it again."

"You are," Perrin said firmly. "You've been worthy all along. You were just carrying too much grief to see it."

He closed his hands around the stone, and tears slipped past his control. He didn't hide them. He let them fall, glimmering in the glow of the Star-Stone.

For a moment, Perrin almost reached out to wipe them away—but stopped herself. This wasn't a wound she could heal. It was one he needed to feel.

She settled for standing close enough that their shoulders brushed. "Take it. Keep it safe. For Tuspin. For your father."

Garantuke nodded, swallowing hard, the tears still falling. And in that instant, she felt his choice again—not just to go with her, but to let her in.

One of the Contrary Men lingered there, hat askew, his beige vest torn. Unlike the others, he hadn't dispersed with the crowd. He hovered, uncertain, like a shadow that didn't quite know where to fall.

Perrin stiffened, her staff rising instinctively. But the man didn't attack. Instead, he shuffled backward a few steps, then forward again, as if caught between two commands. His eyes flicked to her, then away, then back again with a searching intensity that made her skin prickle.

"Why is he still here?" Perrin whispered under her breath.

Garantuke stepped subtly in front of her, protective, though the man only lifted a trembling hand—as though asking permission to follow. No words came out. Just that strange backward gait, and a look in his eyes that was neither hostile nor free.

"Leave him," Garantuke muttered. "He's broken from Malum's hold but not whole enough to trust."

Perrin hesitated. Something about the man's gaze tugged at her chest, like a half-remembered dream she couldn't place. But when she tried to read him deeper, he turned sharply away, melting into the shadows of the corridor—yet not so far that she couldn't sense him trailing after them at a distance. The one that called her "Friend."

She shook herself, deciding not to push it. There were bigger things to face now. Still... a part of her couldn't shake the feeling that this particular shadow was meant to stay with her.

Word spread quickly through Tuspin that Perrin was leaving. By the time she, Garantuke, and the Contrary Man stepped into the cavern's open heart, nearly the entire village had gathered. The glow of the root-bridges cast soft light over the crowd, painting their faces with warmth and sorrow in equal measure. Eric's former followers pushed the car from the fortress down to Tuspin. Others brought back those things that were stolen from the villagers of Tuspin. Garantuke restored the Star-Stone to an approaching elder. "I shall place it back on the Hall of Scrolls," said the elder.

Selena stood with her arms crossed, but her eyes glistened with pride. Kimilo bowed low, her movements crisp, controlled, but the tremor in her voice betrayed her. "Do not forget what Miketo showed you—patience first, always."

"I won't," Perrin promised, though her chest tightened as if the words themselves were a goodbye hug.

The elders approached, their lined faces solemn. One lifted his staff, vines curling faintly along its shaft. "You came to us reckless. You leave... chosen." His voice cracked like dry wood, but the reverence in it sent a shiver down Perrin's spine.

Then Moonshadow appeared for the last time, drifting into view as if she had always been standing just beyond the light. Her gaze moved between Perrin and Garantuke, lingering longest on the Contrary Man that had followed them back. "Paths don't end when you leave a place," she said, her tone layered with meanings Perrin couldn't yet untangle. "They only twist into roads you have not walked before."

Perrin tried to thank her, but her throat tightened too much to force out the words. Instead, she lifted her staff in silent salute.

The villagers parted to form a path to the Allekanu exit, one of the passages out to the world above that had been reopened when Malum fell. The villagers bowed to

Perrin, their silence heavier than any roar of approval could have been. It wasn't rejection. It was mourning, and hope, braided together.

As they walked, Perrin glanced back once more. Tuspin glowed like a dream behind her—bridges alive, crops humming faintly, the people who had scolded her, saved her, and made her into something new.

For a moment she thought she might run back, beg to stay. But then she felt Garantuke's hand brush hers, the Contrary Man's uncertain shuffle at her side, and the staff's steady hum reminding her of who she had become.

She faced forward. The path home waited.

Luda ran up to Perrin and presented her with a painted figurine of Perrin with her staff and Garantuke with his obsidian weapon. "This was the gift that I had asked her to make," said Garantuke.

Perrin was in awe with its exactness. It seemed like Perrin and Garantuke in miniature. Perrin looked up at Luda. "Thank you. I shall treasure this forever." Perrin and Luda reached out to hug each other. They exchanged whispers no one else could hear. Luda then hugged her cousin again. This time, Perrin didn't mind.

The car sat where the freed followers had left it, its once-proud paint dulled with dust and scuffs from the underworld's stones. Perrin brushed her hand over the hood, frowning at the faint tremor that ran through her arm. It felt strange, this machine from her teacher's world, looking so out of place here in Tuspin's glow.

"I should drive," Perrin said, glancing at Garantuke with a hopeful grin. "I mean, I've watched enough videos. How hard can it be?"

Before Garantuke could answer, the Miketo staff gave a low hum in her hand — not a word, not even a whisper, just a clear pulse of disapproval. She groaned. "Oh, come on! What, now it doesn't trust me with wheels?"

The staff pulsed again, firmer. This time, Perrin knew it was a no.

Then, the Contrary Man stepped forward. His hat was crooked, his movements still jerky, backward and halting. Yet when his hand brushed the driver's side door, the car almost seemed to accept him, its metal frame vibrating faintly at his touch.

Perrin froze. "Wait—you're kidding. Him?"

The staff's hum shifted, softer now, almost... approving.

The Contrary Man slid into the driver's seat with that same backward shuffle, fumbling at first with the wheel, then steadying, as though some buried memory was surfacing through the fog of Malum's control. He didn't look at Perrin, didn't speak, but the way his hands gripped the wheel with surprising confidence made her chest ache with questions she wasn't ready to ask.

Garantuke opened the passenger door, frowning but saying nothing. He gestured for Perrin to climb into the back. She did, muttering, "This is so unfair. My own staff thinks I'm a traffic hazard."

The engine coughed to life, echoing through the cavern. Villagers stepped back as the headlights flared, stark against the bioluminescent roots and glowing fungi. For a moment, Perrin pressed her face to the glass, trying to memorize every curve of Tuspin: the bridges of living roots, the golden-winged butterflies, the people who had both scolded and saved her.

The path ahead yawned dark, the Allekanu corridor stretching like the throat of another world.

The Contrary Man shifted the car into gear, and with a jolt, they began to drive toward the surface. Perrin clutched the seat, heart pounding—not from the motion, but from the unshakable sense that the strangest part of her journey wasn't behind her. It was still waiting.

CHAPTER 14: RETURN TO THE SURFACE

The car rolled up the cracked asphalt drive just as the final bell rang, the school building exhaling a flood of students. Backpacks bounced, sneakers slapped the pavement, and chatter swelled into a roar. Perrin shrank into her seat in the back, her face burning as heads turned. The missing car—*the* missing car—was gliding right into the school parking lot with her inside it.

Of course, the real spotlight wasn't on the car. It was on the driver.

The man in the top hat sat stiffly at the wheel, collar pulled high, brim shadowing his face. He parked with surprising steadiness, though his hands twitched against the wheel as if unused to stillness. A ripple of laughter ran through the crowd.

"Who's that—Willy Wonka's creepy uncle?" a boy called, snickering.

"No, seriously, he looks *exactly* like Wonka," another

girl chimed in, loud enough for Perrin to hear. "Top hat, weird vibes. Did you, like, bring back any candy?"

Perrin slid lower in her seat, groaning. "Great. Just what I needed—free advertising for the circus."

Garantuke, sitting tall in the rear seat, stared out at the crowd with his usual steel calm, completely unfazed. If anything, he looked ready to leap out and take on the mob of gawking teenagers. That only made things worse. Perrin imagined the captions already popping up on social media: *Perrin Roberts, back from the dead, brings model boyfriend and Willy Wonka look-a-like to school. Epic cringe.*

As the Contrary Man cut the engine, silence spread in ripples. The car's hood ticked as it cooled, every metallic snap echoing louder than the crowd. Eyes fixed on them. Whispered guesses buzzed like flies. Perrin pressed her forehead to the glass, wishing for Tuspin's glowing caverns over this spotlight.

Her stomach dropped. The hardest battles weren't with villagers, Miketo, or Contrary Men. They were right here—facing her classmates again.

The circle of students thickened, Mengelu Dinkh standing smug in the middle, phone held aloft like a trophy.

"Well, this should be fun," she crowed. "Watch Perrin Roberts *steal* Mr. Gasker's car keys. No excuses this time."

She tapped play.

The video flickered to life. The grainy footage showed

Perrin moving stiffly, her eyes clouded, her hand jerking across Mr. Gasker's desk to snatch the keys. Eric leaned into frame, his voice a velvet snare: *"Bring me the keys. Now."*

The sound carried over the hushed crowd. Perrin's breath caught—her shame about to drown her again—

"Hold it right there."

The students parted as Principal Hollis pushed through, jaw set like stone. Behind him strode Mr. Gasker, sleeves rolled, he took the keys from the Contrary Man.

They both watched the screen. Watched Eric's voice, clear and commanding. Watched Perrin's blank expression, her puppet-like movements.

"That's not how she usually is. Something is definitely wrong with her," Mr. Gasker barked. "That's *him*," Gasker said as Eric's face showed on the screen. "My car, my keys —he compelled her."

Principal Hollis folded his arms, gaze sweeping the crowd like a spotlight. "This absolves Perrin Roberts of any wrongdoing. What you've just witnessed is coercion. She will not carry the blame for being forced."

Mengelu's smirk collapsed. "But—but she still—"

"Enough." Hollis's voice cracked like a whip. "Do you want me to review your record for spreading defamation, Miss Dinkh?"

The girl paled, shrinking back into the crowd.

"The boy who did that to me is locked in the trunk," Perrin told Principal Hollis. Gasker hit the trunk button and personally lifted Eric out.

The silence that followed wasn't just from the students. It was official. Perrin's chest ached, but for the first time since this nightmare began, it was with relief.

The crowd stayed hushed even after Principal Hollis moved off, muttering about calling the Police. Mr. Gasker gave Perrin a short, almost fatherly nod before following, his car keys jingling at his belt.

Then Rosha broke through the ring of students. Her braids were half undone, eyes wide and wet. "Perrin," she whispered, and then louder, "Perrin, I'm so sorry." She grabbed Perrin's arm like she might vanish again if she didn't hold tight.

Keri wasn't far behind. Her usual swagger was gone, replaced with guilt that made her voice trip. "We—we thought you really did steal Gasker's keys. We didn't even *ask* you. We just believed what everyone was saying."

Perrin's throat tightened. She wanted to snap, *Yeah, thanks for leaving me to twist in the wind at the end of rope.* But Rosha's grip trembled, and Keri's eyes shone, and the lump in her chest cracked.

Even Taloni walked up, she looked horrible, she bowed her head and said, "Perrin, you can punch me in the face as much as you want."

"Just... don't do it again," Perrin muttered.

Rosha nodded fiercely. "Never. I swear it."

Keri offered a crooked smile. "Yeah. We're your idiots for life. If you'll still have us."

Taloni's head lifted in shock. "Ah, I really wanted you to punch me."

Around them, other classmates murmured, awkward apologies tumbling out. The same voices that had mocked her now stumbled over *we didn't know,* and *we were wrong.*

Perrin's cheeks burned, not with shame this time, but something stranger—something like being seen again.

The squeal of tires split the murmurs. A squad car swung into the parking lot, lights flashing, siren clipped short.

Mr. Gasker flagged toward him and turned Eric over to them.

For the first time, Perrin felt the tide shifting. The car was back. Her name was clearing. And Eric was in custody, not hurting her or anyone else anymore.

By the time they reached her house, Perrin's nerves buzzed worse than they had in the arena. Facing Eric had been one thing; facing her mom was another.

The front door jerked open before she could knock. Pandra stood there, arms folded, eyes flashing the way they always did when she'd stayed up worrying.

"Perrin Roberts." Her mother's voice cut sharp, but it cracked at the edges. "Do you have *any idea* what I've been through—"

Perrin launched forward, burying her face against her mother's shoulder before the lecture could finish. The scent of cinnamon and laundry soap hit her nose, and suddenly she was twelve again, hiding from thunder.

Pandra froze, then slowly, carefully, wrapped her arms around her daughter."You scared me half to death," she whispered, voice breaking. "You disappear, and then there's talk of the police, and that boy—"

"It wasn't me, Mom. Eric... he—" Perrin swallowed. "They know now. Everyone saw. I'm not in trouble anymore."

Pandra pulled back just far enough to search her daughter's face. She touched Perrin's cheek like she was making sure it was real. Then she hugged her again, fierce this time.

Behind them, the doorframe creaked as the Contrary Man loomed, brim pulled low, staying half in shadow. Pandra's eyes flicked to him, her brows drawing tight.

"And who," she said slowly, "is *that*?"

Perrin opened her mouth, but no words came.

Before Perrin could stammer an answer about the Contrary Man, the porch filled with footsteps. Rosha, Keri, and Taloni crowded close, whispering and giggling behind their hands. And at the center of it all, standing awkwardly tall in the doorway like he'd rather be facing a Belofez than Perrin's mom, was Garantuke.

His broad shoulders nearly brushed the frame, his dark eyes fixed straight ahead, as if refusing to flinch would help. In Tuspin he looked like a warrior. Here, under the suburban porch light, he looked impossibly out of place—half legend, half teenage dream.

"This," Perrin said, voice cracking with both pride and terror, "is... um...Garantuke."

Rosha's jaw dropped. "*That's* your boyfriend?"

Keri made a sound somewhere between a laugh and a gasp. "Perrin, you didn't tell us he was—" She gestured helplessly. "—basically a statue that moves."

Taloni just crossed her arms, glaring in theatrical jealousy. "Not fair. Totally unfair."

Garantuke blinked at the attention, then inclined his head with grave seriousness. "I am honored to meet Perrin's family and companions."

The girls swooned audibly. Perrin wanted the porch to swallow her whole.

Pandra raised one eyebrow, cool and sharp. "Boyfriend, hmm?"

Heat flooded Perrin's face. "Mom!"

Garantuke glanced at her, confused. "Is that... not the right word?"

The porch erupted in laughter, her friends practically melting in a puddle of envy, and Perrin buried her face in her hands.

While Perrin's friends were still whispering and gawking at Garantuke, the man in the top hat slipped quietly past them all, like a shadow no one wanted to claim. He stepped into the living room, shoulders hunched, brim pulled so low it nearly covered his nose.

Perrin followed him with her eyes, uneasy. He didn't sit, didn't speak—just lingered near the window, one hand twitching at the edge of his vest. The houselights painted him in warm gold, but he still looked like he belonged in the wrong century, dragged forward against his will.

Rosha leaned close to Perrin, whispering, "Why's he dressed like that? I thought you fell underground, not back in time."

Keri giggled, too loud. Perrin elbowed her, but the heat in her cheeks wasn't only from embarrassment. She could feel the man's attention—even with his face hidden, even when he didn't move.

Pandra crossed her arms, gaze narrowing. "Perrin. Why is that man in my house?"

"He—he helped us," Perrin said quickly. "He... he's lost. He needs a place to stay until he finds his way home."

The man stirred, muttering under his breath. Words slipped out backward, garbled and fast, like water rushing over rocks. None of her friends understood, but the sound made Perrin's stomach twist with an odd familiarity.

"See?" she added, forcing steadiness into her voice. "He can't even talk straight. He's... he's broken. We can't just throw him out."

Pandra's frown deepened, but she didn't press further —not yet. The man in the top hat turned his head slightly, as if waiting for Perrin's approval. She gave the smallest nod, and his shoulders loosened a fraction.

The air shimmered before anyone knocked or rang. One heartbeat the room was just a living room—couch, lamp, family clutter—and the next, Moonshadow stood in the doorway as if she had always been there.

Her skin glowed a faint, otherworldly blue under the ceiling light, her long hair drifting like it was underwater. To Perrin's friends, she must have looked like a dream half-remembered from some old legend.

Grace gasped. She was already coming down the hallway, shawl clutched at her chest. Her eyes widened, tears brimming instantly. "Moonshadow."

Moonshadow inclined her head, calm as moonlight. "Graywun."

The name hit like a gong. Perrin's breath caught—her grandmother, called by the name whispered in stories told her when she was young. For a moment, Grace looked younger, straighter, the weight of her years lifting as she stepped forward and took Moonshadow's hands.

"I never thought we'd meet again," Grace whispered. "Not after..." Her voice cracked, lost in memory.

"Time divides, but truth remains," Moonshadow answered. "Your line still carries the flame." Her gaze shifted toward Perrin, a flicker of recognition that sent a shiver down Perrin's back.

Rosha clapped a hand over her mouth. "It's *her*," she whispered to Keri and Taloni. "The Moonshadow. The hero from my family's stories. I—I can't believe she's real."

Keri leaned over with wide eyes. "Your grandma hangs out with cultural superheroes?"

Taloni snorted, half in disbelief, half in awe. "Of course she does. Figures."

Grace and Moonshadow stood together in the center of the room, two legends brushing away time. Perrin couldn't shake the sense that this moment mattered— that something bigger than the living room walls was happening, and she was at the center of it.

For a few blessed minutes, the room buzzed with warmth—Grace and Moonshadow speaking softly, Rosha nearly fainting from excitement, Keri and Taloni whispering a running commentary that Perrin tried to ignore.

But the man in the top hat never moved from his shadow by the window. He fidgeted with his gloves, muttering under his breath in that backward spill: *".ereh evah yeht doof fo dnik tahw rednow I"* It grated on Perrin now that everything else felt normal. He didn't belong here, not like Garantuke standing so tall in the light, not like Moonshadow glowing softly beside Grandma Grace. He was an interruption, a puzzle that refused to solve itself.

"Take off the hat," Perrin said suddenly. "It's rude to wear in a house."

His shoulders stiffened. He gave the tiniest shake of his head.

Perrin stepped closer. "You can't just skulk around in my house like some weirdo magician. Hat. Off."

He tucked his chin, clutching the brim tighter. The stubbornness of it sparked something sharp in her. With a frustrated huff, she reached out, batting at his hand to knock it away.

He jerked back, fumbling, muttering even faster. She swatted again, this time smacking the back of his hand with a sharp slap. That sound caught Pandra's ears. She saw the incident unfolding, and then caught a glimpse of his face.

"Perrin, stop hitting your father!"

The room froze. Pandra's voice cut through it like a bell.

Perrin's breath caught. Her hand still hovered near the hat brim. Slowly, painfully, the man lifted his face just enough for the light to catch him.

Grace's gasp echoed Pandra's. Moonshadow only smiled faintly, as if she'd known all along.

Perrin's vision blurred. The face was older, worn, eyes haunted—but she recognized the line of the jaw from photographs in dusty albums. Her throat worked around the word.

"Daddy?"

Bill Roberts gave a small, awkward wave, half-shy, half-broken. His voice, still twisted backward, spilled the sound: "*YddaD.*"

Perrin's tears came fast, hot and unstoppable. She

threw her arms around him anyway, top hat and all.

For the first time since falling into the shaft, she felt whole.

The living room felt too small to hold it all—Moonshadow's quiet glow, Grace's trembling joy, Pandra's sharp relief softened into tears, Bill's, the Contrary Man's, awkward, broken presence under the top hat, and Garantuke towering behind it all, silent but steady as stone.

Rosha pressed both hands over her heart like she might burst. "Perrin...you're living in a fairy tale."

Keri fanned herself dramatically. "Correction: she's *starring* in one."

Taloni rolled her eyes, though her grin betrayed her. "Ugh, we'll never hear the end of this at school."

But Perrin barely heard them. Her gaze was locked on her father's face. Even twisted with the strange backward murmurs, even weathered by years stolen away, he was here. Not a ghost. Not a story. Here.

"Welcome home," she whispered, her voice catching.

Bill Roberts nodded once, solemn, as if the words were a vow he didn't quite know how to keep yet.

Pandra drew Perrin close again, then reached for Grace, pulling three generations into one fierce embrace. Moonshadow rested a hand above them, like sealing an ancient promise.

Behind them, Garantuke shifted, his eyes soft. He met Perrin's gaze, and for the first time, she didn't feel pulled in two directions—Tuspin and Arizona, duty and love. Somehow, impossibly, she had both.

Perrin wiped her eyes, laughter bubbling up through the tears. "I'm not stupid," she murmured, almost to herself. Not anymore.

And for the first time, she believed it.

The End

ABOUT THE AUTHOR

C. S. Dexter

 C. S. Dexter has been writing since he was a small boy. He impressed his teachers at school, he told stories to his friends, he wrote for other people, he wrote for the University he graduated from, but it was when he went to the Netherlands and told a story to a six-year-old girl, named Opal, that he learned that stories could have power. He found this little girl smoking in the city of Lelystad and told her a story about another little girl, named Opal, that smoked cigarettes. When he was done, Opal pulled out her pack of cigarettes and threw them away, promising never to smoke again. When he last enquired if Opal was keeping her promise never to smoke again, her mother reported that Opal hadn't smoked since that day.